"What's the story on this Doug chap?"

Jack's voice was demanding.

"I see no purpose in discussing him," Kaarin said coolly. "So, if you don't mind...."

"Ah, but I do mind. Did you love him?"

Kaarin thought briefly of refusing to answer, then shrugged. "I thought I did...once."

"What does he do?"

"He's a...writer," she replied cautiously.

"Never get involved with writers; they're terrible bastards," he chuckled. "I'd have thought you'd know better, considering your job."

"Let's just say it's not a mistake I'm likely to repeat," Kaarin replied. "So in future, Mr. Collier, I'd be much happier if you'd keep your kisses—and your hands—to yourself."

"Actually," he replied with a knowing grin, "you wouldn't."

VICTORIA GORDON
is also the author of these
Harlequin Romances

2427—THE SUGAR DRAGON
2433—WOLF AT THE DOOR
2438—THE EVERYWHERE MAN

Many of these titles are available at your local bookseller.

For a free catalogue listing all available Harlequin Romances and Harlequin Presents, send your name and address to:

HARLEQUIN READER SERVICE,
1440 South Priest Drive, Tempe, AZ 85281
Canadian address: Stratford, Ontario N5A 6W2

Dream House

by

VICTORIA GORDON

Harlequin Books

TORONTO • LONDON • LOS ANGELES • AMSTERDAM
SYDNEY • HAMBURG • PARIS • STOCKHOLM • ATHENS • TOKYO

Original hardcover edition published in 1981
by Mills & Boon Limited

ISBN 0-373-02458-4

Harlequin edition published February 1982

Copyright © 1981 by Victoria Gordon.
Philippine copyright 1981. Australian copyright 1981.
Cover illustration copyright © 1982 by David Craig Artist Ltd.

All rights reserved. Except for use in any review, the reproduction or utilization of this work in whole or in part in any form by any electronic, mechanical or other means, now known or hereafter invented, including xerography, photocopying and recording, or in any information storage or retrieval system, is forbidden without the permission of the publisher, Harlequin Enterprises Limited, 225 Duncan Mill Road, Don Mills, Ontario, Canada M3B 3K9. All the characters in this book have no existence outside the imagination of the author and have no relation whatsoever to anyone bearing the same name or names. They are not even distantly inspired by any individual known or unknown to the author, and all the incidents are pure invention.

The Harlequin trademark, consisting of the words HARLEQUIN ROMANCE and the portrayal of a Harlequin, is registered in the United States Patent Office and in the Canada Trade Marks Office.

Printed in U.S.A.

CHAPTER ONE

KAARIN sat across from her 'uncle' William, sipping idly at a glass of excellent Moselle as she tried to build up the courage to drop her bombshell.

The words danced theatrically on the tip of her tongue, all too often threatening to spill out in disorder as she struggled to arrange them properly. Three times she'd started to make her statement, but each time the words had tripped into confusion and she'd been forced to stop, rearrange them, and seek an opportunity to begin again.

It was all so very difficult. Though technically not really an uncle, William Cleaver was a distant relation on her mother's side. More important, he was her employer, her landlord—and her friend. Telling him she wanted to leave her job, leave Sydney in spite of all he'd done for her, gave Kaarin an overwhelming sense of betrayal and guilt.

But it must be done, and with a firm breath she resolved to try yet again.

'Uncle . . . I . . .' William Cleaver raised one manicured, slightly pudgy hand in a gesture that halted the effort even before it was properly begun.

'Not before we've finished eating,' he said sternly, only the twinkle in his eye showing that he wasn't being stern at all.

'But . . .'

She got no farther; again the imperious gesture and this time even his eyes showed sternness.

'Later, I said. I flatly refuse to ruin a perfectly good lobster Thermidor with a discussion of your plans to run off back to the bush and leave me without the best personal secretary I've ever had.' And a broad grin spread across his rather pudgy face, giving him the appearance of an especially benevolent Buddha.

Kaarin was speechless. He *knew*! All her recriminations, all her guilt and worry, and he'd known all along. She should have expected it. Shaking her head in a gesture that fanned soft, ash-blonde hair around her head like a broad halo, she grinned back at him.

'You're unbelievable,' she whispered. 'It's no wonder you're so successful—you read people's minds.'

'Anyone who can't has no business in publishing,' he retorted. 'Authors being what they are, you have to be able to read their minds just to get any sense out of them. But I'm sure you've found that out for yourself during the past year, perhaps a little too well?'

Kaarin blushed slightly, tearing her pale blue eyes from his glance and staring uncomfortably down at the oysters Mornay which were cooling untouched on the plate before her. He knew. He even knew about Doug and what a fool Kaarin had been in believing the young writer's wholly convincing words of love everlasting.

'Eat your oysters; young Patterson isn't worth wasting good tucker on,' said William Cleaver. 'Of course I could have told you that in the beginning, but I reckoned you'd have the good sense to get rid of him before any permanent damage was done, and I was right. Wasn't I?'

'If you mean before I hopped into bed with him, yes,' Kaarin replied candidly. 'But only just, if you must know. Frankly, I rather wish you *had* warned me off.'

He shrugged. 'Some people learn best by their own mistakes,' he replied around a mouthful of lobster. 'I knew you'd come good in the end, you country girls are a helluva lot smarter than some of these airy-fairy types can ever imagine.'

Country girl! In two words he'd struck at the heart of all Kaarin's problems, and she smiled despite herself at the accuracy of the publishing magnate's thinking.

'Well, this country girl doesn't feel so terribly smart about anything,' she replied. 'Honestly, Uncle Bill, coming to Sydney was the worst mistake I could ever have made. Worse than Doug, even. I didn't much like the place when I was here at school, and I'm afraid I like it even less now, despite all you've done.'

'You're wrong, Kaarin,' he replied. 'If you hadn't come, you'd always have wondered. This way you know for sure and you can go back to Dubbo, or Woop Woop or wherever, and *know* that the city's not your thing. Be thankful; a lot of people in this world haven't even that much.'

'Oh, I *am* thankful,' Kaarin replied. 'You've been absolutely marvellous and I really feel I've learned a great deal as well, although I'll still feel guilty about leaving you.'

'Not for a month or so, in any event,' was the reply. 'We'll have to get somebody training to replace you, and I absolutely refuse to do without you until we get this problem with Collier worked out.'

'Worked out? You can't even find the man,' Kaarin retorted. 'I know what I'd do about the elusive Mr Collier if I were you, Uncle Bill—I'd send him off to another publisher and call it damned good riddance.'

She bobbed her head in a gesture of annoyance and then attacked her oysters with an unexpected return of appetite.

Bill Cleaver shook his head sadly. 'Ah, Kaarin, how innocent you are sometimes,' he sighed. 'And to think I actually said country girls were smart! One does *not* send off the goose who lays the golden eggs to somebody else's goosery, or whatever they call it. Jackson Collier has brought in more money for our firm than most of our other writers combined. And he'll do so again, once he's over his little snit, or whatever it is that made him go bush in the first place.'

'You mean Neridah Gregg? Or don't you believe the Sunday papers' account of their traumatic and ill-fated love affair?'

'Do you?'

'I ... I don't know,' Kaarin replied honestly. 'I've yet to meet the famous Jackson Collier, don't forget. But Neridah Gregg is an extremely beautiful woman. If half what the papers say is true, I suppose it's possible that Collier's gone off to sulk somewhere after being rejected.'

Bill Cleaver's bark of laugher was startling. 'Not on your Nellie,' he snorted. 'Neridah's got beauty, brains, social position and money, but she's not woman enough to send Jack Collier off to any hermitage, I'll tell you that. I don't know what Jack's up to, but it won't be sulking over any woman. Let's just hope that whatever it is, he doesn't forget that today is when his new book is due on my desk.'

'But what if it isn't?'

'Tomorrow's another day,' Cleaver shrugged. 'Besides, today isn't over yet, and I've got a fair bit of faith in old Jack. He's an old pro, that lad, not the type of fellow to let a bit of woman trouble put him out of the game.'

'A minute ago you said that wasn't it at all,' Kaarin protested. 'I don't think you're as sure of your Mr Collier as you make out.'

'Let's put it this way, if it had been him you were involved with instead of young Patterson, I wouldn't have stayed on the sidelines,' Kaarin's 'uncle' retorted.

'Your confidence is overwhelming,' she replied acidly. 'Not that it matters in any event. I've learned my lesson quite well enough, thank you, and next time I'll find some nice, sensible grazier. No more writers.'

'You'd change your tune in a hurry if he walked in

and took a fancy to you, my child. Wait until you meet him before you start making rash statements.'

'I've seen his picture and read his books, which is quite enough,' Kaarin retorted. 'He strikes me as being incredibly arrogant—and not very considerate in the bargain or he'd have been in with his book already.'

'Arrogant? My very word, he's arrogant,' William Cleaver replied. 'Or at least that's the way he appears. Probably the result of having spent the last twenty years beating off the girls with a big stick. But then, you being an ever-so-sensible country girl, I suppose you'd sit there and tell me he doesn't attract you in the least.'

'Being an honest country girl I'd have to admit he's quite handsome, at least in his pictures,' Kaarin replied. And admitted privately that 'quite' was an understatement. Her mind conjured up the picture of Jackson Collier she'd selected for the jacket of his upcoming book, a head-and-shoulders shot of the man staring off into the distance, sunlight casting halos around the wind-blown tangle of coffee-coloured hair, sloping, hooded eyes so darkly brown they were almost black and adorned with sloping brows that pointed towards a deep crease between his eyes. His nose was hooked and prominent, with finely-carved, flaring nostrils.

Jackson Collier was ... thirty-seven, she thought. And looked it, too. His brow was furrowed and strong lines drew down from the high-bridged nose to the sides of his mouth and the deeply cleft chin. There were pouches beneath; the deep-set eyes and, overall, the man had a slightly dissipated look.

'Probably from beating off too many girls,' she muttered, then looked up to chuckle at the startled expression on her uncle's face. 'Sorry, I was thinking out loud, I guess,' she said.

'Hummph! I hope you never think about me like

that,' he replied. 'Maybe you've learned more than I thought. Anyhow, it's time we got back to the salt-mines, my girl. We won't get rich sitting here.'

'No, just fat, which I can do without,' Kaarin replied, sliding lithely to her feet. At five foot nine without the advantage of her two-inch heels, she towered over her diminutive 'uncle', who took great delight in saying he only kept her around because he'd never seen so much woman in one package before.

The first time, at an author's party where she knew virtually no one, Kaarin had nearly died with embarrassment, but during her year in Sydney she'd come to accept Bill Cleaver's quirky sense of humour because she'd come to love him as dearly as she had her parents, who had both died a year ago as subsidiary victims of one of the worst droughts in Australian history.

It had been a combination of a gastro-enteritis epidemic and sheer hard work that had taken first her mother and then, hardly a week later, her father, who Kaarin thought in her heart had really died of a broken heart at the loss of his wife and the beef herd he'd spent a lifetime building.

For Kaarin, the loss hadn't stopped with her parents; she found out all too soon that their western New South Wales property had been mortgaged to the hilt long before the drought had slowly killed off the cattle and sheep, turning the land she loved into little more than a desert.

She went to the funeral in a daze of disbelief, came out of it almost hysterical with grief, and would have suffered even more but for the kindly interference of Bill Cleaver. He'd swept aside any objections from any quarter, taking Kaarin back to Sydney with him and supervising the disposition of her lifetime home with professional acumen and genuine compassion.

He had taken her into his home, given her the challenge of a position as his private secretary, and gradually helped her to accept her losses and realise that time is indeed a great healer. A mirror near the restaurant doorway showed nothing of the frightened country girl she'd been that one short year before.

Instead, the young woman who looked into the mirror as Cleaver paid the bill was every inch a city sophisticate. Kaarin's silken, pale blue blouse and cream suit was fashionable and striking on a figure few men could fault.

Both of her parents had been tall, as had most of the young men in the district, so Kaarin had grown up with no selfconsciousness about her height. She carried herself tall and proudly on long, shapely legs, shoulders back and head erect. Her crown of flowing blonde hair was thick and naturally wavy, and she'd been blessed with thick, high-arched brows over large eyes of a pale grey-blue. Her face was conventionally pretty, with a straight, finely-shaped nose, a generous mouth and a slightly dimpled chin above a long, slender neck. The features were perhaps a shade strong; she could never be accused of typical blonde vapidness, but overall she was an intensely attractive woman and didn't bother to try and hide it.

Once back at her desk, which nearly filled the anteroom to Bill Cleaver's enormous, book-lined sanctuary, Kaarin found it increasingly difficult to concentrate on her work. What would she do, once her commitment to Uncle Bill had been completed? Where would she go—certainly *not* back to Dubbo, that much was certain.

Perhaps ... perhaps Queensland, somewhere near the coast where the temperate sea breezes and subtropical temperatures made for year-round summer living. A small town, perhaps, not too firmly in the tourist belt, but still linked to the rural values and solidarity she required. She was lost in pleasant if idle speculation when the telephone rang.

'Mr Cleaver's office . . . may I help you?' She spoke into the instrument without coming wholly away from her daydream.

'Is he there?' The voice that rumbled from the telephone had an unusual resonance, deep and solid.

'I'm sorry,' Kaarin replied, slightly surprised by the unusual opening. 'What was it you wanted?'

'I said, "Is he there?"' replied the voice, revealing just a hint of annoyance.

'Mr Cleaver, you mean?'

'Well, of course Mr Cleaver. You did say this is his office, or aren't you sure now?'

'Of course I'm sure,' Kaarin retorted. 'May I tell him who's calling, please?'

'Sure.' The word held a note of haughty contempt, and was followed by a long silence.

'Well?'

'I'm sorry; I asked if I might tell him who's calling.'

'And I said "sure", didn't I?'

'Which tells me absolutely nothing at all,' Kaarin snapped back. 'I can't very well tell him who you are if you don't tell me in the first place.'

'You didn't ask. You asked if you could tell him who's calling, which is a totally different thing. Want to try again?'

'Not especially,' Kaarin hissed into the telephone, 'but I suppose you'll want to continue this silly little game until I do. May I have your name, please?'

'Tell him it's God.'

'I most certainly will not!'

'All right, tell him anything you like, just get him on the line for me like a good little girl. I'm in a phone booth and all your protective little secretarial ways are costing me money.'

'I'm only doing my job,' Kaarin replied firmly. 'Now if you'll just give me your name . . .'

'If I were there I'd give you a bloody good spanking,'

snarled the voice. 'Now will you just get old Bill on the horn for me and stop messing about!'

'Oh! I think you'd better start all over, and clean up your act while you're about it,' Kaarin snapped. 'Mr Cleaver does not like to be disturbed without good reason.'

'And you're supposed to monitor his phone calls and screen his visitors ... I know, I know. Hell, do you change his nappies for him too?'

'I do not! Now are you going to give me your name or ...' Kaarin was cut off by the operator interrupting to ask the mysterious caller to deposit more money. She was sitting, open-mouthed and staring angrily at the telephone, when Bill Cleaver strode from his office and paused to look down at her in some concern.

'Kaarin ... what's wrong?' he asked, eyes straying to the telephone in her hand.

'Ooooh! I've got some whatname on here who insists on talking to you, but he won't give me his name,' she replied hotly. 'All he'll say is "tell him it's God", if you can imagine such a thing.'

'Help! Put him through immediately,' replied Bill Cleaver, scurrying back to his office in obvious panic.

Kaarin, startled by his action, put the telephone to her ear just in time to hear, '... interfering bloody office house-mother. Hey ... you! Are you going to get Cleaver for me or do I have to reach through this telephone and twist your ear?'

'Yes, sir. Right away, sir. Immediately, sir.' Kaarin's anger kicked her voice up several octaves, but she made no attempt to hide it. Instead, she punched the intercom button and said, 'God is on line one, Mr Cleaver.'

'Jack Collier ... where the hell are you, and where the hell's the book you promised me?' Bill Cleaver's voice boomed through into Kaarin's office and she halted in the act of replacing the telephone.

So *God* was the infamous Jackson Collier. Yes, that'd be right. Just exactly his brand of arrogance, she thought. And thrust aside all principles to brazenly listen in on the conversation that followed.

'How are you, Bill? My oath, but you've got that chick well trained! What does she do, guard your office door with a meat cleaver?'

'That book, Jack . . . .'

'Oh yeah, that's what I called . . .' The interruption of the long-distance operator cut off the rest of the sentence, and the following few seconds were filled with the jingling of coins as Jackson Collier once again paid his toll.

'Listen, mate, this is ridiculous,' he said once service returned again to normal. I'm in a phone booth and I'm running out of two-bob pieces after trying to get past your gorgon. I'm on 071-7 . . . so have the darling girl ring me back and we'll discuss this without all the hassles, okay?'

And he hung up without even waiting for a reply, leaving Kaarin livid with anger at the arrogance of it all. She was sitting, still holding the telephone, when the bleep of the intercom brought her back to reality.

'Did you get that number, Kaarin?' asked Cleaver. 'Ring him back straight away before the silly dill pulls another disappearing act, would you?'

Kaarin was able to listen in unashamedly when she rang the phone booth and coolly advised Jack Collier that Mr Cleaver was returning his call, but for the first few minutes she was too occupied in trying to search out Jack Collier's location in the area code section of her telephone directory to really follow the conversation.

It was little consolation, therefore, to have Jack Collier answer her question by replying, 'I'm in Gayndah right at this moment, but I'm staying on the old home place up near Mingo Crossing.'

'Where the hell is that, and what does it have to do with the book you're supposed to be writing?' Bill Cleaver's carefully hoarded anger was beginning to show through in his voice.

'South-east Queensland . . . inland from Bundaberg,' came the reply. 'And the book's written, at least in my head. I could have it done in a couple of weeks with a dictaphone, but I haven't got time. I'm building a house.'

'You're what?'

'You got it. Building a house. And I want to get done before winter, so the book'll just have to wait a bit.'

'The hell it can! You're not going to throw my entire schedule for a loop because of some half-witted building project, Jack. I just can't allow it.'

'Look, Bill, I know how you feel and I'm sorry. But this isn't some half-witted project, it's something I'm damned well going to do and that's that. It is more important to me than this book or any other damn book.'

'Well, it isn't to me. Damn it, Jack, there must be some way we can compromise on this. What about if I send you a typist and she can take it all down on tape while you're working, or in the evenings or something? That way you could keep on with your . . . building, and I'd still get the book. Late, but not too late, maybe.'

'Oh, that's all I need. Listen, mate, I came up here to get away from women; I don't need to start importing them. Besides, it's pretty primitive up here. I'm living in the old place, and it's rough, believe me. No, it wouldn't work out. Besides, I don't want some spunky little secretary type hanging around and getting in the way.'

'Have you got any better idea? Short of totally destroying your contract. Damn it, Jack, you just can't do this. It isn't ethical.'

'Oh . . . hell! All right. It'll only be a week or two, maybe less if it rains. But don't send me any damn junior typist, Bill. I mean that. In fact, why don't you send up your gorgon? She's got no sense of humour and probably fat ankles and a moustache, from the sound of her, but I'll bet she's efficient as hell. She could probably help me build the house and edit the rough draft as well.'

Kaarin's gasp of outrage was, fortunately, hidden beneath Bill Cleaver's snort of laughter.

'Helluva good idea. Fantastic!' he chortled. 'Shall I put her on the line and you can give her the directions, Jack?'

'Hell, no. I don't want to have to talk to the old trout until I'm absolutely forced to,' was the astounding reply. 'What's this . . . Tuesday? It'll take her three days, even on her broomstick. Have her meet me at Ban Ban Springs at noon Sunday. And tell her to bring lots of tape recorder batteries; I've got the power on here, but it's erratic as hell. Can she cook?'

'Like a dream,' Bill Cleaver replied honestly.

'On a wood stove? I doubt it, but she couldn't be much worse at it than I am. Anyway, you'd better give her plenty of expense money and a decent vehicle, because she'll have to stay in a pub at Gayndah and there's fifty kilometres of bad road between there and my place. Unless of course she wants to camp with the possums or share my dog's kennel.'

Kaarin stifled a snarl of anger. That last bit had been positively evil. The absolute nerve of the arrogant, opinionated twit! She was a hair's breadth from shouting something terribly rude into the telephone when he suddenly concluded his conversation and abruptly hung up.

Kaarin walked angrily into her 'uncle's' office to find Bill Cleaver doubled up with laughter, gasping it out in great hoots and guffaws, tears streaming from his eyes. The sight was too much for her tattered nerves, and seconds later she was sprawled in a chair across from him, her own laughter mingling with his in a contagious whirlwind of hilarity.

'You . . . you don't honestly mean to send . . . m-me out there, d-do you?' she finally managed to gasp.

'Thick ankles, moustache and all,' Bill Cleaver replied in an explosion of words that deteriorated immediately into renewed laughter.

'I . . . I won't go,' she stammered, struggling to control the fresh laughter that bubbled up inside. 'I . . . I . . . couldn't!'

'Of course you'll go. Think of the . . . the surprise when old Jack . . . sees you,' Cleaver managed to say. 'Oh, I wish I could be there to see it!'

Both of them dissolved in helpless laughter that subsided first in Kaarin. 'Seriously, I couldn't go,' she began, only to be interrupted.

'Of course you must go. Jack has asked for you— you, specifically,' Bill replied. 'It's only for a couple of weeks—think of it as a holiday in the country. In fact, I'll even rent you a camper van and you can take a fortnight when it's over and go touring on your own. How's that?'

'Well, at least it would give me a place to stay,' she replied cautiously. 'I mean, I'd have to have some place private to sleep, and the idea of driving back and forth to . . . whatever that town is, twice a day . . . that's quite ridiculous.'

And then she thought to herself in absolute surprise, My God, I'm actually seriously considering it. I must be quite mad, utterly mad!

'It wouldn't work, honestly Uncle Bill . . . the whole thing is just too ridiculous for words,' she said then.

'Not at all. In fact the more I think about it the better I like the idea,' was the surprising reply. 'I mean, you're not going to have to worry about Jack ... er ... well, you know. Not unless you encourage him or something. He's actually a proper gentleman at heart. And at least maybe we can determine just what it is that's bugging him so badly ... why he's gone all strange and hermit-like. It really is a fantastic opportunity, Kaarin.'

'For you, maybe, but I'm not so sure about my own involvement in this,' she replied. 'I mean, it's obvious, surely, that Collier isn't going to welcome me. In fact, I could see him becoming quite hostile about the whole thing.'

'No! Once you're there, he'll accept everything. He'll have to, he's got a contract with us.'

'Ummm ...' Kaarin was torn between frank scepticism and the overall challenge of the thing.

Her 'uncle' looked up at her and turned on one of his Buddha-like smiles. 'Come on ... what's the absolute worst that can happen?' he asked. 'You get to ... wherever the hell it is you're supposed to meet him and he flat out rejects you. So you've had a nice little tour of the country and come home by a different route. It's still a good holiday.'

Kaarin shook her head. 'I don't suppose you'd even understand if I told you it isn't being rejected that I worry about,' she mused. 'Collier is an arrogant, smarmy and thoroughly objectionable person, as far as I'm concerned. I don't like him, frankly doubt that I ever shall, and if the two of us are stuck together for a fortnight on some isolated property we'll more than likely be at each other's throats before it's over.'

'Piffle!'

'Easy for you to say, but if you get another phone call cancelling his contract and dissociating him from you for ever, then don't blame me.'

'Sorry, dear girl, but I most definitely would,' replied Bill Cleaver. 'Jack Collier is a man, and he's just as susceptible to a beautiful woman as any other man. I have no doubts about your ability to bring him to heel, and I expect you to do it.'

'Well, I think you're asking far too much,' Kaarin replied. 'I'm simply not the right person for this job. You should send...' And in the long silence that followed she realised her mistake. Send whom? There wasn't anyone else who would even think of going on such an absurd mission.

Bill Cleaver beamed at her. 'Ah, the penny drops,' he chortled. 'You may not be the right person for the job, dear Kaarin, but you're certainly the *only* one. Goodness, girl, stop looking so apprehensive! Think of it as an adventure, which it very likely will be.'

'More like a disaster,' Kaarin muttered ruefully. 'All right, I'll go, I suppose. But I give you fair warning that I may very well never return. And you're paying all expenses, including the fanciest camper van I can hire and a fortnight's holiday when it's all over. Somewhere nice, like Surfer's Paradise.'

'Done! And believe me you won't regret it,' Cleaver cried.

'I'm already regretting it,' she retorted. 'Now if you'll excuse me, I have forty thousand things to do if I'm to get away on this insane assignment first thing tomorrow.'

'What's to organise? Only the camper, which will take ten minutes. I'll even do that for you; I've got several good contacts in the hire field.'

'Uncle Bill, your problem is that you think too much like a man,' Kaarin replied with a shake of her head. 'Yes, you organise the camper; I'll do the myriad other tasks and I'll see you at home for dinner, provided I get everything finished in time.'

She just made it, arriving in an avalanche of parcels and cartons at just the moment Bill Cleaver drove up in a shiny new Toyota camper van.

'How's this?' he asked with a broad smile. 'Even a nice baby-blue colour to match your eyes.' Then his eyes caught the enormous pile of parcels in the back of Kaarin's ancient and battered Mini.

'My God! All this for a couple of weeks in the bush? Looks like you've bought out half of Sydney.'

Kaarin laughed. 'Hardly any of it is for the couple of weeks in the bush,' she chuckled. 'For that all I'll need is several pair of jeans and a few tops, which I already have. Most of *all this* is resort clothing, thank you, for the holiday you promised me when this Collier insanity is over with.'

'And I imagine you'll need it,' Cleaver replied with a mischievous grin, then sobered immediately at the light of alarm in Kaarin's wide-set blue eyes. 'Only joking ... only joking ... don't panic,' he cried.

He spent the next hour helping Kaarin load the new van, which he revealed he'd actually bought, rather than hired, and then insisted upon taking Kaarin round to a nearby Japanese restaurant for a sumptuous farewell dinner.

Throughout, he devoted himself to assuaging the rising doubts she felt about the entire Collier project, and most especially to allaying the fears raised by his earlier remark about her needing a holiday when it was over.

It would have been almost humorous if Kaarin hadn't been so increasingly certain that he was deliberately lying about everything except the significance of her expedition.

Every time she tried to raise the more serious questions that welled up inside her, her uncle-employer brushed them aside with uncharacteristic aplomb. It wasn't until quite late, and with the unexpectedly sobering effect of several glasses of *saki*, that he made a startling admission.

'Kaarin, we need Collier's next book. *Need* it,' he

said gravely. 'It's not that we couldn't survive without it, but I have to admit that the security of another Collier book in the pipeline would be especially welcome right now. So please give it your very best effort. Jack may very well be difficult, at least at first, but he's a professional and so are you; once you've got that established between you I'm certain everything will work out superbly.'

'Why do I have the feeling I've been led down the proverbial garden path?' Kaarin asked ruefully. 'This is going to be the most well-deserved holiday I've ever had, provided I survive to enjoy it. But what you've said now worries me—not the Collier bit, but the rest. Are you sure you can actually afford to send me off on an expensive holiday, presuming of course that I manage to secure the manuscript?'

'Compared to what one of Collier's books brings in, I could afford to give you six months on the Gold Coast, if it was necessary—no, forget I said that,' her uncle laughed. 'Seriously, let's just say the financial implications of the book are tremendous, but the holiday won't make a great deal of difference one way or another.'

'You're sure?' Kaarin's apprehension was reaching full growth now, fanned like a growing flame by the admission of just how important her expedition might prove to be. She could feel the tension mounting inside her, a tension that would become worse instead of better until the manuscript was secured and in her uncle's hands.

'I'm positive.' He grinned convincingly. 'Now let's be off home so you can get a decent night's sleep before starting off on your adventure. Of course you'll wait until after the morning peak-hour traffic before leaving.'

'Not a chance,' Kaarin replied. 'I'm going to grab what sleep I can and be long gone before daylight. If I can get up through Windsor and cut across to pick up the New England Highway I can make better time and maybe even cut the distance a bit, although it isn't going to matter a great deal with more than twelve hundred kilometres to travel.'

'You're certain you'll be able to make it by noon Sunday? I forbid you to go taking any chances, or driving too long at a stretch,' Cleaver said frostily.

'Oh, stop it, Uncle Bill! Sometimes you're positively antiquated,' she replied. 'It's only about eight hundred miles overall, and I could manage that in two days if I had to. Even puddling along, which is what I fully intend to do, I should be there in plenty of time. Maybe even early.'

She paused then, a look in her eye that might have been pensive but wasn't. 'In fact I just might be *sure* I'm early, and if I can locate your Mr Collier I'll save him the trouble of driving out to meet me.'

CHAPTER TWO

SHE didn't manage to surprise Jackson Collier as she'd planned. The people who ran the combined motel-café-service station at Ban Ban Springs had never heard of Jackson Collier or anyone even remotely matching his description, so Kaarin was left to spend a day and a half amusing herself in the relative serenity of the tiny oasis.

Ban Ban Springs, as a community, barely qualified for the description of a wide place in the road. It was, in fact, a 'T' intersection graced only by the service station complex and a rudimentary picnic site adjoining the springs themselves. To the south, via the Burnett Highway, lay Brisbane; the Isis Highway led northeast to Childers and the Bruce Highway that followed the Queensland coast, while north-west lay Gayndah, Mundubbera, Eidsvold and Monto.

The historic springs themselves, even in this year of inconsistent rainfalls and severe drought conditions through much of New South Wales and Queensland, supported a magnificent huge lagoon with a resident population of water birds and kangaroos.

Only a stone's throw from the highway junction, the springs glistened with dark, life-giving water and resounded throughout the day with the songs of the many birds. As she waited with growing nervousness for Collier's arrival, Kaarin spent her time feeding the various ducks, coots and other birds and reading all of Jackson Collier's books.

Her drive north from Sydney had been uneventful and, once she struck the New England Tablelands and began to drive through all-too-familiar reminders of the drought that had taken her parents, tremendously depressing. Even here at Ban Ban Springs, where explorer Thomas Archer had halted with relief during his exploration of the Burnett region in 1848, the oasis-like quality of the springs and lagoon couldn't totally negate the harsh, barren dryness of the slightly rolling country around.

Reading Jackson Collier's earlier novels did little to dispel Kaarin's troubled mood. In her apprehension about meeting the man, she found herself reading into his work tremendous currents of sensuality and hidden violence that she had never noticed in earlier readings.

On the Saturday night, huddled into the fold-down bed of the camper-van with all doors secured and the van itself parked as inconspicuously as possible, she had nightmares for the first time in almost a year. And they were horrid, vivid nightmares, black fantasies in which the hawk-like visage of Jackson Collier rode like an avenging conqueror over the trampled remains of Kaarin's own serenity—a raping, pillaging bandit of spectacular proportions.

One was enough to bring her upright in the narrow bed, screaming soundlessly into the darkness in a mute reply to the shouts and cries of a group of larrikins having their weekend booze-up in the far corner of the picnic grounds. Kaarin shivered, thankful she'd been out of sight within the van before their arrival.

She was even more thankful when a roving highway patrol chivvied the carousers off a few minutes later, allowing her to at least try and seek a relaxing form of sleep for the brief period remaining before the cacophony of song from the springs announced the imminent arrival of another five a.m. sunrise.

Kaarin rose with the sun, her eyes tired and grainy from her fitful night but unable to bother trying to sleep with her mind so overflowing with apprehension. Knowing she had hours yet—too many hours—to wait for her impending noon appointment, she slipped into her oldest pair of jeans, faded and snug from years of use. A light cotton shirt and an elastic band round her hair completed the outfit, and before the sun was fully awake Kaarin was halfway round the large lagoon, one hand filled with old bread for the waterfowl and her eyes carefully surveying the ground in case of a wayward snake.

But by seven o'clock she was already bored beyond belief, so bored that she decided to splurge on a breakfast cooked by someone besides herself, and after locking up the camper she hiked across to the motel complex and indulged herself with steak and eggs, several rounds of toast and two cups of black, steaming coffee.

That filled in the time nicely until eight o'clock, but once back in her camper she found the heavy breakfast riding uneasily upon her tension-laden stomach.

The next few hours were a continuing nightmare. Kaarin tidied up the camper, unpacked and repacked every single item of clothing she'd brought with her, checked the water and oil levels and the tyre pressures in the van, read half a page of Jackson Collier's last book, made a cup of tea, read another half a page—or was it the first half over again? Her mind simply refused to function except at the most primitive level.

Subconsciously, however, it functioned all too well, especially when it came to visualising alternatives for her upcoming meeting.

... 'Good morning, Mr Collier. I'm Kaarin Amos. Mr Cleaver sent me.'—'Well, good morning, Miss Amos; I'm very pleased to meet you. You're not ... quite what I expected, but I'm sure we'll work very well together.'

... 'Good morning, Mr Collier. I'm ...'—'I don't care who you are, so long as you can take dictation and type quickly without getting in my way.'

... 'Good morning, Mr Collier. I'm ...'—'On your way back to Sydney, that's what you are. And when you get there, tell Bill Cleaver . . .'

On and on it went, moving from the patently ridiculous to the proverbial sublime. It accomplished nothing, except to clench more tightly the growing knot in Kaarin's stomach, but it did pass the time, after a fashion. At least until the noon deadline approached, arrived, and *passed*.

But as one o'clock, in its turn, also passed without a sign of the spectre that was Jackson Collier, the knot in Kaarin's tummy began to twist and squirm as tension smouldered into anger that quickly was fanned into a white-hot rage that increased with each passing minute.

Oblivious to the heat of the sun on her bare head, she paced round and round the caravan, eyes burning and every sense somehow alert and alive. Her mind no longer conjured up variations on the meeting; instead it plotted all manner of unholy and vicious revenges. Collier couldn't have survived most of them and indeed Kaarin couldn't have survived their implementation, but the thoughts were raw fuel for her anger.

If he's not here by two o'clock then to hell with him and good riddance, she thought at ten minutes to that hour, but when the appointed deadline arrived she reneged, and instead of driving southward again she stalked across to the restaurant and sat glowering into a cup of steaming black coffee.

She was halfway through the coffee when a flicker of movement outside drew her eye, and she looked up to see the most battered, decrepit-looking utility in the entire world squatting beside the gas pumps. Beside it stood a tall, lean, almost cadaverous figure in a T-shirt and shorts so grotty as to match the truck itself. Ragged, uncut hair melded into a curling, tobacco-coloured beard and a face tanned almost as dark as the hair itself.

It was impossible for Kaarin to hear the conversation

between the lean, bronzed figure and the pump attendant, but she didn't need words to interpret the thumbed gesture towards the springs, where her camper sat in isolated obviousness.

For an instant she was stunned. Surely this ragged, scrubby-looking scarecrow couldn't be ... but then the figure turned, profile silhouetted by bright glaring sunlight. It was! There could be no mistaking that hawk-like beak of a nose, and even the scruff of untrimmed beard couldn't quite disguise the thrusting, determined chin.

Kaarin half rose from her seat, then obstinately settled down again as the tall figure waved some gesture at the gas attendant and strode away towards the highway intersection and the lush greenery of Ban Ban Springs. She couldn't help but notice the long, muscular legs, the springy, arrogant stride and the squareness of broad, rippling shoulders beneath the questionable cover of the ripped and stained T-shirt.

A fine figure of a man indeed, she thought. Arrogant devil! Well, he could damned well wait until she'd finished her coffee. *Then* she'd walk over quite calmly and deal with the illustrious Mr Jackson Collier.

A slow smile, sufficiently wicked to draw a startled look from the waitress, played about Kaarin's shapely mouth as Jack Collier strode up to thump on the door of the empty van. Kaarin didn't need to hear the words to interpret his comments at receiving no answer to his summons, nor to read the display of anger he showed as he turned to survey the area around the springs, dark eyes searching restlessly.

Kaarin sloshed down the remainder of her coffee, grimacing slightly at the coolness of the dregs. Then she rose slowly to her feet, casually rummaged in her handbag for sufficient change to pay the score, and just as casually left the cool sanctuary of the restuarant to stroll with studied nonchalance towards her van.

Jackson Collier was out of her sight as she walked slowly across the hot bitumen of the roadway and then on to the relative coolness of the grassed picnic area, but as she reached the corner of her van he suddenly stepped into view from behind it, standing like a sentry before her with muscular bronzed arms folded insolently across his chest.

She looked up haughtily to meet a pair of piercing dark eyes that suddenly seemed to encompass her, driving first into her own alert and cautious gaze and then roving down the curves of her slender body with an expert's appraisal. One eyebrow cocked in accentuated surprise and the mouth hidden beneath the untrimmed beard suddenly opened in a wry smirk to reveal white, even teeth.

Jackson Collier stood as if rooted to the spot, then his grin faded and once again his eyes roved hungrily, possessively over Kaarin's body. Then, without warning, they lifted to claim her own eyes, locking her to him as if by a bar of rigid light.

'My ... very ... word,' he breathed, his voice so low she barely heard him. 'And what, pray tell, are you?'

There was an insolence in the voice, but more than that. There was also an assertiveness, an undercurrent of rank maleness. His every sense seemed to radiate the dominance, the aggressive possessiveness of a conqueror. Here was what every conqueror in history must have looked like when first assessing a future domain ... there was the vivid, glittering eye of Genghis Khan, or Attila the Hun, or Alexander the Great.

Kaarin shivered inside, but it was a tremor that showed neither in her chilling blue eyes nor in the calm but icy voice with which she replied.

'Obviously, Mr Collier, I'm a gorgon. That's what you specified, did you not?' She continued without waiting for any sort of reply, and now her voice began to carry not only the ice in her dignity but the fiery rage in her stomach.

'I am also, I would point out, *on time*, something of which you could hardly be accused. Or is punctuality just another little irrelevancy to you, along with contractural obligations, common courtesy and a reasonably professional attitude towards your work?'

She clamped her mouth shut then, jaw muscles trembling as she lifted her head even farther to glare up at him. And when he didn't speak, she snapped out at him yet again, this time with a quivering, near-breaking-point snarl in her voice.

'What's the matter, Mr Collier, misled by the lack of fat ankles and moustache? Well, don't let it worry you; I am, I assure you, thoroughly efficient and capable of transcribing your deathless prose into a saleable manuscript.'

The beard made it difficult to assess his reactions. It hid the strong lines so evident round his mouth, a mouth that in his photograph was wide, generous and strong. A mouth that closed over strong white teeth that suddenly were revealed as he grinned ever so slightly.

'Are you done?' Again that terribly soft, inflectionless way of speaking; it was a blunt, direct question asked without warning from the dark, fathomless eyes.

Kaarin started to speak, but her mouth was barely open when, as if taking her momentary silence for reply, Jackson Collier's lips moved once again.

'Right, let's go.' And he was moving, stepping forward so quickly that Kaarin started in alarm, but already he was past her, shifting his broad shoulders and trim, narrow hips in a graceful, subtle gesture as he strode past her without another word. When she had caught her footing and turned, he was striding away towards the service station, walking with a lithe, comfortable stride that belied any impression Kaarin might have made.

She stood, speechless, as he paused to pay for his gas, then slipped into the driver's seat of the disreputable old utility. How incredible! How frightening, she thought, her anger lost in the gulf of his obvious indifference.

And then she was scrambling for her own driver's seat as he swerved his truck out of the driveway and headed north-west towards Gayndah without a single glance in Kaarin's direction.

He drove expertly, and so quickly that Kaarin was forced to extreme concentration just to keep him in sight. A few kilometres up the road he turned off on to a narrow gravel track and sped along it with no apparent regard for the dust and gravel that was thrown up behind him. Kaarin's van, rather less designed than the ancient untility for such roads, churned along in his wake with its youthful driver white-knuckled at the wheel.

At one or two points the gravel gave way to short stretches of bitumen, then suddenly the dust cloud Kaarin was pursuing slewed to the right and became noticeably lighter in colour as Jackson Collier's vehicle moved from the gravel track to an even narrower one of pure dirt. Grimly, she followed, although now she was forced to slow down and his elderly ute ploughed out of sight amidst the twists and turns of the narrow rutted track.

Beside her, massive, sky-reaching gum trees waved gnarled arms in the breeze, stretching out rooted feet to try and trip up the labouring van. Kaarin's arms ached from the effort of steering when she rounded a final turn in the track and found herself at the edge of a broad clearing around a falling-down, weathered set of buildings and stock yards.

The house was the worst, a forlorn-looking structure

with a sagging hip roof and stumpy support legs beneath it that seemed barely adequate to hold up the sprawling verandahs.

Jack Collier's truck was way off to the left, sagging in the tall grass beneath the questionable shade of a gum tree on the crest of an outcropping. Beyond it, the ground fell away swiftly towards what Kaarin presumed was some sort of watercourse.

She halted her van just inside the clearing, and after the briefest of surveys, turned also to the left, trundling over the uneven ground to park in the shade of yet another forest giant of a eucalypt. Jackson Collier, standing beside his truck with one hand nuzzling the snout of an excited dog, made no gesture to guide her, but merely stood idly watching as she parked the van.

As Kaarin reached for the door-handle, the dog gave an excited yip and loped over to sit just outside her van, staring up at her solemnly through eyes like the bottom of a beer bottle. It was a mottled blue colour, mingled with dark patches that comically covered one eye, one hip and half its tail, but Kaarin saw nothing comical in the dog's attitude. The animal was a bitch, obviously heavy in pup yet still showing every attribute of the finest type of Queensland Blue Heeler. It wasn't a large dog, but the short, slightly wavy coat revealed sturdy musculature and the broad, strong jaws and clean lines showed up the purity of its breeding. This dog was close to being the best of its type Kaarin had ever seen, and the stillness of its tail was warning enough.

Kaarin had grown up among cattle dogs, most of them blue heelers or a mixture of cattle dog and kelpie, and she knew only too well the virtues of the breed. Outstanding workers, instinctively using the best of introduced capabilities from an ancestry most experts thought to hold substantial dingo blood, they were also fiercely protective, one-man dogs.

Once out of the van, Kaarin knew she would be committed. Either the dog would grant her grudging acceptance or she faced the ordeal of having it snapping at her heels with powerful jaws at every possible opportunity.

And Collier, the devil, knew it! Kaarin looked up to see a grin flicker through the beard, a grin that then widened into an inviting, mocking, devilish smirk. He made no move to either provoke the dog or pacify it, and Kaarin snarled inwardly at the callous challenge of it all.

She shot him a glare that should have withered the grass at his feet, then slowly shoved open the van door and stepped down, moving slowly but positively as the bitch lurched upright, meeting her glance with those awful, expressionless eyes as it stood there, staring aggressively.

'Well, aren't you a fine-looking specimen?' Kaarin asked in a low, soothing voice. 'And I'll bet old whatshisname over there is too busy building his stupid house to even feed you properly in your delicate condition.' She bent almost in a curtsey, one hand slowly extending to give the dog her scent but with her eyes locked on those amber orbs.

'Don't panic, old girl. Take your time,' she crooned. 'But you'd better make up your mind to be nice to me, 'cause I'm a better cook than he is, and you're going to need plenty of tucker pretty soon, I reckon.'

From the periphery of her vision, she caught a flicker of movement as the tail twitched, just once, and she let half a smile emerge as the dog's massive muzzle stretched slowly forward until it almost touched her hand.

'Yes, you're a good girl . . . and very well trained too I think,' she crooned. 'Although I really can't imagine what misfortune teamed you up with a character like that one standing over there smirking at us. He thinks you're going to have me for lunch, you know? I'll bet he's kept you hungry for a week just waiting for me. But we'll fool him, won't we? Ah yes, we will.'

A mottled tongue slid out to caress her fingers and the tail began to scythe gently to and fro. Kaarin slowly straightened then, still holding the dog's eyes. 'Okay, let's go,' she said softly, and then, more firmly, 'Heel!'

And with a confidence she really didn't feel, she turned her back on the dog and stepped smartly towards where Jackson Collier lounged against the side of his truck, the smirk now replaced by a bland, blank expression that told Kaarin nothing at all.

This was the supreme test, she knew, resisting the urge to look back at the dog. She was either going to have a victory, for whatever it was worth, or a painful nip on the ankle.

Jackson Collier stood impassive at her approach, only his eyes moving as they slid from Kaarin to the dog and back again. Kaarin resisted the temptation to follow his gaze, and instead marched resolutely ahead until she stood squarely in front of him, noticing from the corner of her eye as the bitch slid around to hunker silent beside the man's tall, slender figure.

His eyes were almost as expressionless as those of his dog, although of a darker, deeper brown. He stood looking into Kaarin's eyes for what seemed like an hour, then his mouth quirked into something that might have been either sneer or smile.

'All right,' he said softly, and without warning reached out to take her left hand in his right, kneeling then to bring both of them down to the dog's level.

'You're a proper fickle little bitch, by God, you are,' he drawled as the dog moved in to snuffle against where their hands and scents mingled. The tongue reached out to flick at each exposed wrist, then withdraw behind ivory fangs as the bitch grinned up at each in turn. Collier straightened then, releasing Kaarin's hand but leaving on it the brand of his touch, the heat and the feel of his calloused fingers in an indelible mark.

'Well, get your gear and let's get at it,' he said then, and turned away to pluck a shovel from the bed of the truck before striding down over the brow of the ridge.

'I don't believe this,' Kaarin muttered to herself, standing as if rooted to the ground while she watched Jackson Collier slowly drop out of her vision. Then she shook her head, shrugged her shoulders, and marched back to the van to collect tape recorder and shorthand notebook. The blue heeler trotted amiably beside her, laughing up into her face as if amused by her total confusion.

Kaarin stepped over the crest, following almost exactly in Jack Collier's footsteps, and halted with a gasp of pleasure and surprise. Below her, perhaps twenty feet lower than the original homestead site, sprawled a small, perfectly level beach of perhaps an acre in size. It was surrounded by huge, spreading gums interspersed with clumps of wattle and the occasional spear-topped grass skirt of a black-boy tree, and the far edge cropped away still further in a series of flood plains to where a clean, bright river tinkled over jumbled rocks before falling into a broad, swirling pool. And everywhere it was green, a lush, beautiful green that contrasted amazingly with the relative dryness of the bush above.

Slightly to the left of centre, a series of stakes and strings and fresh-cut sod marked the foundation lines where Jack Collier's house would stand, and the man himself, taut muscles flexing beneath his sun-darkened hide, was heaving out fresh cuttings of soil in a series of practised, easy movements. The shovel blade dug in, shoulder muscles flexed as he bent to lift it, depositing the soil neatly beside the tidy trench that was slowly eating its way round.

Off to one side, a huge assortment of broad, flat river

stones was stacked with unexpected neatness, and still farther over was a raft of great, fresh-cut logs, some still gleaming with sap where the bark had been sliced away. There was a sense of neatness and order that somehow blended perfectly with the serenity of the site, and Kaarin felt herself responding to the calm—until she reached Jack Collier's side.

'All right,' he said without preamble. 'Chapter Three. Par ... Fletcher's fingers tangled in the woman's hair, which closed and flowed around his hands like seaweed ...'

Kaarin lost four words as she made the mental transition to Chapter Three. What happened to the first two? she wondered, but didn't have time to ask.

Jack Collier never stopped his rhythmic work, bending and lifting and bending again, his voice dictating the story with a soft, melodic tone that matched the movements of his muscular body. It was almost hypnotic, and Kaarin, stepping silently along beside him as she backed up the tape with her neat shorthand squiggles, found her eyes focusing somewhere between the notebook and the tangle of Jack Collier's rough-shorn mane of dark hair. Her senses became attuned to him, picking up the clean, fresh scent of his perspiration, the glistening of it upon his dark skin, the flexing of muscle and the stretch of hard-hewn, twisting wrists.

He never once looked up at her, never paused for an instant in his deliberate, almost caressing excavation of the trench in which he stood and moved.

He moved like a well-oiled machine, some form of android with a human exterior but a steel and cable internal structure that couldn't ever tire, but gradually his voice took on a life of its own, lifting and falling, calling up inflections of hatred and passion and ... love, as his story unfolded word by word, phrase by phrase.

The dictation was swift, perhaps a hundred words a minute, and unrelieved by any pause for thought, but the hypnotic quality of his voice was such that Kaarin felt no strain, no weariness as her fingers raced to keep up. At the warning bell from the dictating recorder, indicating the approaching end of the cassette, he fell silent, but still he didn't look up as Kaarin hurriedly turned over the cassette and turned a fresh page of her notebook.

The shovel rose and fell in a mystical rhythm, not even breaking when Kaarin said, 'all right', and his voice came alive again, picking up where he'd left off without any hint of uncertainty.

They went through the second side of the tape, and only then did he pause. His eyes rose to meet Kaarin's, dropped to the face of the watch on his left wrist, then rose again. 'An hour to dark,' he said in an expressionless monotone. 'You'd best go and start tea now.'

Her mouth dropped open in astonishment, but Jackson Collier didn't see it; he'd already leaned down again to his work, picking up the rhythm of economic, almost musical movement.

Kaarin's mouth closed, opened again, but no sound emerged. The ability to speak seemed to have been swept from her as the red tide of outraged anger swept up from inside. She stood immobile, eyes following the movement of Collier's lean, trim body, then snapped her mouth shut and turned to stomp angrily up the hillside to her camper.

She flung the tape recorder and notebook down on the folded-down bed, then turned to stare at her image in the mirror. Eyes snapping with suppressed rage glared out from a face paled by the shock of Jack Collier's rudeness, but as she stood there, colour flowed back—a colour heightened by her hours of standing in the sun.

'Start tea . . . indeed! Not very likely, Mr high-and-mighty Collier,' Kaarin whispered to her reflection. She shook her head angrily, sending waves of shimmering blonde hair into a whirlwind around her head. 'Not very likely at all!' she cried even louder.

And turning to the tiny refrigerator, she fumbled out a half-bottle of sweet Moselle, a chilled glass, and sat determinedly down at her table, eyes boring through the window as she stared at the ridge beyond which Jack Collier was presumably still working.

Twenty minutes later the bottle was empty along with the glass, and Kaarin was slumped over the table, face buried in her crossed arms as the combined effects of sun and wine began their work.

Later still, she opened her eyes and weakly raised her head as a knock thundered on the door of the van, but before Kaarin could move the door opened to reveal the tall, looming figure of Jackson Collier, a scowl creasing white lines across his sunburnt forehead.

'No tea, eh?' he grunted almost absently, and then his eyes widened as they took in Kaarin's flushed complexion and wide-staring eyes.

The room seemed to swim around him, and Kaarin made a frantic effort to reach her feet as her stomach rolled inside her, rearing and kicking as if she'd swallowed a demented horse.

'Oh . . .' she whispered. And then, 'Ooooohh!' as she lurched to her feet, jaw clamped shut, and plunged towards the doorway where Jack Collier's figure stood like an obstacle. He stepped aside lightly, one hand out to steady her as she stumbled through and got her feet on the shifting, rolling ground just as her stomach erupted in spasms.

She was only dimly aware of hands at her waist and neck, steadying her as the world tumbled and churned with her retching, and later as something cool swept across her brow, then down the lines of her neck, her cheek, and finally across her flaming, burning face and quivering mouth.

'Ooh!' she whimpered, and then tumbled into a darkness where something strong and strangely gentle cradled her body, lifting her like featherdown as consciousness retreated.

Then came the nightmares, a grinning, devilish dog with empty amber eyes and teeth like ivory scimitars ... warm rains that burned where they touched her naked body, and cold, icy seas that swept over her in waves of agony ... the piercing eyes of a wedge-tailed eagle, perched above her as it stared down at the pallid, pulsating whimpers of its next dinner.

... And eyes, dark and deep and ... knowing. Eyes that swept over her with the cruelty of a rapist, violating her with their touch. Eyes that changed, shimmering with a soft, tender compassion, a warmth that soothed and protected her, cradling her against the ravages of the hot rain and the chill seas.

... And hands, sometimes angry, hurting, trapping her wrists like handcuffs. But also soothing, mother-like hands which stroked and pampered her, bringing an incredible feeling of security and safety.

And a voice. It was that which finally brought her back from the nightmares. It was a voice like thick, creamy chocolate fudge, monotonous and yet rich with emotion and life. On and on it went, drawing her into the tale it related of passion and love and fearful dangers and terror and tenderness. The voice stirred her, lifting her from the lassitude within to the broad richness of life in the real world.

Kaarin's eyes flickered open, weakly responding to the lure of that voice, to the dim light and the figure— the naked, muscular figure of the man who sat by the table, his voice lilting like faerie music as he talked.

Naked? No, not naked. He wore a pair of faded, cut-off jeans that moulded to his narrow hips as he rose, switched off the recorder, and strode over to stand like a bronzed god above where she lay. A hand reached out in the sudden silence, touching her burning forehead like a kiss. Eyes, dark and alive with compassion, met her own and dark caterpillars of eyebrows squiggled above those eyes.

Then the fingers touched ever so gently upon her eyelids, closing them softly, and the voice returned, driving into her feverish brain with a curiously insistent finality.

'Sleep ... sleep ... everything is all right ... you're safe now ... just sleep ... sleep ... sleep ...'

And it was morning. Or so she imagined when the crow of a nearby rooster scrabbled over her senses like fingernails on a blackboard.

Kaarin's eyes popped open, then widened with alarm. Where was she? The half-light of piccaninny dawn showed her only a corner of a table, an incredibly ancient table, and she slewed her head round to see first a yellowed window, then dark wooden walls, the table again, and finally the sooty exterior of an antique wood-stove complete with built-in water heater.

Kaarin thrust herself upright, then slid back beneath the coverlet with a low cry of alarm. She was naked, her breasts thrusting out around an angry, scarlet valley that glistened with moisture. She reached up, wonderingly to touch herself, and recoiled at the equally red arm that raised itself into view.

Then, lightly, she touched her face, felt the tautness there, the oily coating that seemed somehow soothing, and she closed her eyes and let her arm drop limply down on to the coverlet.

'My ... God!' she muttered, and then her eyes flashed open as a creaking floorboard announced that she was not alone. Memory flooded back as the tall figure of Jackson Collier, straight out of her dreams in only his faded shorts, moved into view.

He said nothing, merely seated himself beside her on the bed and reached out gently to raise her head to the tall glass he held. Kaarin's lips fluttered to clutch at the rim, parting to let the chill iciness of the water pour into her parched mouth. Gratefully, greedily, she slurped at the water, oblivious to everything until an icy trickle between her breasts made her gasp with surprise and alarm.

She reached out then to push Jackson Collier away, but he only shook his head wearily and reached down to lift the coverlet so that it concealed her breasts.

'Don't fuss,' he said quietly. 'I'll get you some more water.'

And he was gone, stalking silently from her sight to return seconds later with yet another ice-chilled glass of the life-giving fluid. This time he raised a finger in caution, forcing Kaarin to drink slowly, savouring the coldness, the liquid, fluid spread of the water through her parched tissues.

'Enough for now,' he said then, eyes and face impassive as his voice. 'Could you eat?'

Eat! The very thought of it brought her stomach into revolt, churning wildly to screw up her face in a gesture of disgust.

'I thought not,' he said calmly. 'Rest now; we'll see if you feel differently at lunch-time.' A huge hand reached out to cup her chin gently.

'And I mean *rest*,' he said. 'You so much as set foot outside this house and your bottom'll be redder than your face. Count on it!'

And he was on his feet again, striding towards the doorway. Where he stopped and turned to favour her with a slow, almost gentle smile.

'You sure do go to extremes to get out of cooking,' he chuckled. 'Hope you've got something fit for breakfast in your camper, 'cause *I'm* starving.'

And he was gone. Just like that.

Kaarin closed her eyes, half certain it was all some strange, hallucinatory dream. But when she opened them a minute later she was still in the same bed, in the same room.

The realisation of what must have happened struck her then like a physical blow. Sunstroke! And from the look of her arms and the angry red valley between her breasts, she could hardly bear to think of what her face must be like.

She thrust aside the coverlet and slid her legs out of the bed, gratified to realise that she hadn't been stripped entirely naked after all. She was still wearing her jeans, which immediately began to chafe uncomfortably where her sandals had left her feet unprotected from the sun. They too were burned a dismaying shade of crimson.

'Oh, how incredibly stupid!' she cried, rising swiftly to her feet and trying to ignore the giddiness in her stomach. 'Bathroom. Surely he's got a bathroom here somewhere,' she muttered then, moving dizzily around the small room until she spotted the appropriate doorway.

Inside, an aged mirror told its horrific tale. Her face was a scarlet fury, with the sunburn right up into the roots of her cornsilk hair and running down in a long spur where the throat of her blouse had been open. Her neck was likewise badly burned, and even the top of her head felt tender.

And dirty! The dust of the journey and sunburn as well was too much to face. Kaarin surveyed the rather primitive shower arrangements, then threw caution to the wind. Anything would be better than the way she was.

A moment later she was sighing with relief as cool, cool water cascaded over her body in a cleansing, replenishing torrent.

It was a temporary but worthwhile agony to gently work some borrowed shampoo through her long hair and sponge away the dust and grime of travel, and to lather soap very gently into the burned areas of her body.

'Use all the water you like; it comes straight up from the river,' said a voice that startled Kaarin so badly she almost fell. With soap in her eyes and her hair tangled across her face, she could only squeak out her alarm.

'What are you doing?'

'Bringing you something to wear,' was the calm reply. 'Need any help?'

'Certainly not. Would you please get *out* of here!' she replied hastily.

'I'm not in there; I'm outside the window,' Collier replied. 'There's some more sunburn cream there as well; see that you use it. And then get back to bed. You've had a helluva burn and you're nowhere near as fit as you think right now.'

There was a pause, in which Kaarin scrubbed desperately at her hair in an attempt to see where he was—and more important, what *he* could see, and then the voice came again.

'I'll be gone for a couple of hours and I want your promise that you'll stay inside ... out of the sun. And no work ... none! Is that a promise?'

'Yes ... yes,' she replied angrily. 'Anything you like, but please go *away*!'

Only silence answered her.

She heard the rumble and rattle of his ancient utility as she stepped from the shower, peering nervously around the bathroom as she did so. Incredible! There on the window ledge was her handbag, the light cotton caftan she often used as a nightgown, a tube of sunburn cream, her toiletry case, and ... unbelievably ... a steaming cup of tea.

She shook her head in wonderment. What an astounding gesture, she thought, then grimaced at the return of some of the vague memories of the night before. Had Jackson Collier undressed her, carried her into his house, his bed, sponged away the marks of her sickness, applied sunburn cream to her face, her arms, the deep cleft between her breasts? Her face would have reddened at the thought had it been able, and she shivered at the incongruity of it all. But he must have done all these things. And, modesty aside, done them very well indeed.

She reached for the tea, mouth twitching as she recalled his remark about getting out of cooking. Obviously he had some sense of humour, though it must be buried deep in that imperturbable exterior. A sense of humour, and—memory said—a great deal of gentleness and compassion as well.

'All of which you seem to hide very well,' she said aloud to his aura, which seemed to permeate the room. 'But thank you, anyway.'

She drank the tea then, and welcomed its soothing influence upon her still-rebellious tummy. Then she spent a painful twenty minutes gingerly working her comb through the masses of towel-dried blonde hair that seemed to make her scalp's sunburnt tenderness intensify.

She soon found out that Jackson Collier had been all too correct in his assessment of her fitness. Just the effort of combing out her hair seemed to dissipate all of Kaarin's energies, and it was several minutes before she could even summon the strength to return to the narrow kitchen bed where she had spent the night.

It took several minutes more to apply new lashings of sunburn cream to her face, neck and arms, after which another short rest seemed like an admirable notion. Secure in the covering of the tent-like cotton caftan, Kaarin leaned back against a pair of heaped-up pillows and closed her eyes . . . just for a moment.

The creaking and groaning of the elderly utility returning woke her to the startling realisation that her moment must have been more like an hour, and she had barely got sat up in the bed when Jackson Collier shouldered open the cabin door and sauntered in, his arms filled with parcels.

No word of greeting, not even a smile. He merely walked over to deposit most of the parcels on the kitchen table, then turned and walked solemnly over to stand beside the bed. Silently, he reached down to deposit a wide-brimmed straw hat on Kaarin's head, stepping back as if to admire the effect. It was an amazing hat, with a brim so huge it spread far past her shoulders. Placed on a stick it would have made an excellent beach umbrella, and on her tender scalp its weight was an immediate annoyance.

'Thank you,' she smiled, then reached up to remove the headpiece.

Jackson Collier didn't return either the smile or the thanks. 'You don't leave this house without that on . . . not even to go from here to your camper,' he said firmly. 'Try it, and you won't sit down for a month.'

Then he turned back to the table and tossed several tubes of various sunscreen lotions at her. 'And use these as well,' he said with equal firmness.

'All right,' Kaarin replied acidly. 'Thank you very much—and yes, I've got the message. Do you have any other orders for me, or can I get up and get started on the work I came here to do?'

'Tomorrow,' he replied grimly. 'Today you'll rest. I got a fair bit on tape last night and I'll do enough tonight so that you can work inside. You might as well do it in here; it'll be cooler and less confining than the van.'

'Okay, but really I'm fine, now,' she replied. 'And as I've already slowed things up by being . . . stupid and forgetting about the sun, I really think I should . . .'

'What you should do—and will do—is what you're told,' he broke in. 'You'll stay in the house and you'll rest. You'd be even less use to me—if that's possible—getting yourself sicker than you are.'

And he turned on his heel and strode out of the door, slamming it behind him with no hint of gentleness.

Kaarin got only slight satisfaction in sticking out her tongue at his retreating figure, a gesture so incredibly childish that she was ashamed of herself a few moments later when she thought about it.

But what a rude, arrogant, bullying man he was! Threatening to spank her if she disobeyed his slightest command . . . a threat all the more maddening since she had no doubts he'd carry it out.

'Well, *that* for you and your orders, Mr Collier,' she muttered angrily, raising one hand in a universally rude gesture. 'At the very least I'll do something about this pigsty, and get things organised so that tomorrow I can get busy on your stupid book.'

It was a grand gesture, but a rather useless one. She found on closer inspection that despite the cabin's ancient origins and obvious long abandonment until Jackson Collier had moved in, it was surprisingly clean and tidy. Kaarin managed to find only a few cobwebs to dust away and some tracked-in grit on the time-smoothed wooden floors.

Putting her notes and tapes in order took even less time because Jackson Collier had obviously been one step ahead of her yet again. Stacked neatly were tapes covering the first two chapters of the book, her own work of the day before, and another two full tapes that she presumed carried on after that.

'He must have worked all night,' she mused wonderingly.

'And on an empty stomach, too' said a voice from the doorway. 'Are you up to eating lunch, or do you reckon your stomach will take it?'

'I'm ... not sure,' she replied, striving to recover from the surprise of finding him standing there. Did the man have to move so quietly? she wondered. It was most disconcerting. 'Perhaps I could manage something light,' she said.

'You can have steak, eggs, or steak and eggs together, unless you've got something better in your van,' he said. 'I wouldn't count on it, though; I pretty well cleaned it out at breakfast.'

'That was certainly thoughtful of you,' she retorted. 'I think I'll go over now and see just exactly what you did do, besides eating my food and pawing through my wardrobe.'

And with that she strode angrily towards the door, only to be halted by an enormous hand that reached out to ensnare her arm. She was turned half around, facing away from him, when a slap on her bottom brought her almost clear of the floor with a howl of outrage.

But before she could retaliate, Jackson Collier had jammed the outsized straw hat on her head and stood, grinning wickedly as he held open the door for her.

'Don't say I didn't warn you,' he sneered. 'Next time you'll get a stronger lesson!'

Speechless with anger, Kaarin could only snap her mouth shut and leave the cabin with what little dignity she could muster.

CHAPTER THREE

SEETHING with anger, she arrived at the van to find nothing of the chaos she'd expected. It only served to fan her anger when she found the dishes neatly washed and stacked, not a single article in the van out of place, and the only evidence of Jackson Collier's enquiry into her wardrobe was the caftan she was wearing.

Foodwise, it was a slightly different story. The four chops that would have given her at least two meals—gone. Along with the half-loaf of bread, the litre of milk, three oranges and most of a jar of pickles. Half a rasher of bacon, her small remaining stock of imported marmalade, and a quarter of a jar of olives were also absent.

Fuming, Kaarin gathered up the remainders, a few olives, the pickles, two oranges and a banana, replaced the hat on her tender head, and stomped angrily back to the cabin.

'Here—you might as well finish these while you're at it,' she snarled, shouldering open the door and flinging the food on the table. 'And just for the record, I think you've got a damn nerve!'

'Don't overwhelm me with gratitude,' he retorted. 'Just sit down and wait ten minutes and I'll give you some steak and eggs in return.'

'Yuck! Haven't you got anything else?' she replied. The thought of steak and eggs in her present condition made her stomach turn rebellious.

'Yeah, there's some dog food and some chook pellets, if that suits you,' he replied without looking round from his supervision of the wood-stove's fire.

Kaarin looked round the kitchen, noticing for the first time the huge old refrigerator and the small, compact freezer against the far wall. Without answering him, she strode over and yanked open the fridge.

'My God!' she cried, recoiling in horror. The entire refrigerator was packed from top to bottom with cans of beer. There wasn't room inside for so much as a packet of butter.

She slammed the door and turned to fling up the lid of the freezer, half expecting to find a hindquarter of steer—unbutchered—inside. She was almost right; a moment's floundering among the tidily-wrapped packages revealed only steak, steak and more steak, each packet neatly labelled by the butcher from where it had come.

'Saves a lot of decision,' Jackson Collier remarked over his shoulder, and Kaarin could imagine only too well the smirk that would be on his face.

A sizzle announced the arrival of steak to griddle, and she looked up to find him soberly scrutinising the biggest T-bone steak she'd ever seen in her life. While she watched, he broke four eggs into a huge cast-iron frying pan—one-handed, no less—and stood idly watching as the eggs stared up at Kaarin like evil yellow eyes.

It was too, too much for her delicate stomach. Kaarin fled to the bathroom with Jackson Collier's laughter ringing in her ears. And there she stayed until the sounds from the kitchen indicated that he'd finished eating and was cleaning up.

'I think you're the most callous individual I have ever met,' she said upon re-entering the room, standing hands-on-hips in the doorway and trying desperately to freeze him with her eyes. The effort was largely wasted.

'Okay,' he agreed without a hint of a smile. 'See you later.' And he was gone, striding off to his labours without any sign that she'd managed the slightest impression upon his impervious ego.

The afternoon was agony. Kaarin's bad mood, she realised, was at least as much her own fault as his, but it didn't make it any easier to cope with. She tried to rest, found it impossible, thought about eating and rejected the idea instantly, debated the wisdom of settling down to some typing and rejected that when she walked across to the camper, hat firmly in place, and found that it was like an oven inside. Even with all the windows open, creating heaven for hordes of bush flies, the camper was simply too warm to consider working in during the heat of the day.

At five o'clock, having exhausted all other possibilities, she felt physical assurance returning, if nothing else, and began seriously thinking about dinner.

Jackson Collier had conveniently set two huge steaks out to thaw, and despite her earlier aversion Kaarin found the thought of a hearty meal increasingly tempting.

But not—not ever—the concept of half-raw steak and smirking eggs the way Jack Collier seemed to enjoy them. Ugh! After a few minutes' thought, she scampered across to raid the camper for what few spices and condiments she'd brought with her, angrily determined to put the arrogant Collier in his place by providing at least a semi-civilised meal that evening.

There was enough flour and other requirements for her to put together a small damper, heavily laced with a handful of sultanas she found sulking all alone in the cabin's near-empty pantry, and she raided the henhouse and found almost a dozen fresh eggs for a spicy omelette.

The huge steaks were laid out and slathered with a mixture of sauces which could soak in and provide additional flavour. Whether Jackson Collier would allow her to cook his long enough to make any difference was open to question, but at least she'd have a go, Kaarin thought.

And the next day, typing or not, she was going to have to convince him that a food shopping expedition was top priority.

She had everything ready, the damper baking perfectly in the oven, when the first hint of twilight made her decide it was time to call the lord and master to his dinner.

Kaarin was through the door, indeed stepping off the porch, when a warning bell sounded in her head. That hat! That stupid, outlandish hat. Still, better a moment's inconvenience than a massive war, she thought, and returned long enough to sit it tenderly upon her head.

She walked slowly to the crest of the ridge, savouring the spicy odour of gum leaves and the first light stirring of the evening breeze. How quiet it was, and how peaceful compared to the smoggy, crowded streets of Sydney. Except for the abrasiveness of Jackson Collier, the place was well-nigh perfect.

As she reached the crest, a burst of excited yapping from the blue heeler turned Kaarin's eyes from the work-site, now abandoned, to the edge of the large pool in the corner of the river. Peering from beneath the huge hat-brim, she could see the dog bounding about, and just past it, Jackson Collier in the midst of clambering up on to a high rock that edged the pool.

There was no denying the agility of the lean, bronzed figure as Jackson Collier flowed up the rock like some hunting animal, then paused at the crest, fingers busy at his waist.

Too late, Kaarin realised what was happening, and she had no opportunity to avert her eyes as the ragged cut-offs slid from his hips to leave him standing naked on the rock, his attention on the depths below him. Kaarin didn't bother, then, to look away, but stood in fascinated silence as he prepared to dive into the cool waters of the pool.

The powerful, aggressively masculine figure stood poised for several seconds upon the rock, a motionless, almost primitive statue of elemental beauty. Then, in a single flowing motion, Collier dived from the rock to carve a fluid path through the deep, cold water.

Before he could reach the surface, Kaarin hurriedly turned and ran back from the brow of the ridge, fighting the temptation to stay and watch and knowing it would be no more than the greatest of folly.

She walked back to the house more slowly, once out of Jackson Collier's possible sight, and in her mind was no longer the peaceful vision of silence and gum trees, but the far more stimulating and less peaceful vision of that muscular statue upon the rock.

When he walked into the house a few minutes later, beads of moisture still captured in the dark-curled hair on his chest and in his beard, and carrying his T-shirt although, thankfully, wearing his cut-off denim shorts once again, Kaarin had to force herself to avoid a subconscious reappraisal of the man's lithe, athletic movement and rippling, clean-cut muscular structure.

He entered without a greeting, strolling straight to the refrigerator, where he extricated a can of beer and virtually poured it down his throat. Disposing of the tin, he moved over then to seat himself at the table, which Kaarin had already set in preparation for dinner.

He sat in silence, neither looking at Kaarin nor obviously avoiding looking at her, his eyes almost unfocused as he stared straight ahead of him.

'It will be ten minutes. Would you like another beer?' she asked, almost unwilling to break into his aloof withdrawal, yet bothered by the silence, the lack of any form of communication between them.

For a minute she was afraid he wouldn't even answer her, but finally he slowly swivelled to meet her eyes, and she was startled to see in his own eyes a slow, distinct return from wherever he'd been. 'I'm sorry,' he said, 'did you say something?'

Kaarin repeated herself.

'Ah . . . no, thank you,' he replied, and as he turned away she saw the remoteness sliding back into his eyes.

He's mad! Or on drugs or something. Nobody can just turn off like that, she thought. And shivered inside at the weirdness of his reactions.

Yet when he was faced with the plate of steak, omelette and damper, he seemed normal enough. He politely waited until Kaarin had put her own plate on the table (or was it that he just hadn't noticed his own until then? she wondered) reached over to hold her chair for her (promising?) and then ate with apparent enthusiasm (or was it just a swift, mechanical action?).

But over all, the silence, the remoteness, held sway. And it was, to Kaarin, a spooky, almost frightening silence. Collier spoke not one word until he'd finished every morsel on his plate, and then all he said was, 'Good!'

Then he slid to his feet, padded out to the door after picking up his pipe and tobacco from a shelf on the kitchen wall, and closed it behind him. When Kaarin finally mustered the calmness to check, he was slouched in a chair on the porch, puffing quietly and staring off into space.

'Unbelievable!' she muttered to herself, slamming the dishes around in the sink with quite unnecessary violence as she washed up. 'The man is truly mad! And even more important, he's quite unbearable. I shall never manage a fortnight here; he'd drive me right round the twist with him.'

She was just finishing off when the door opened and Jackson Collier poked his head in, a vague, questioning look on his face.

'Did you feed the dog?' he asked, and the expression was that of a man vaguely trying to remember something important.

'No. Nor the hens, either, for that matter. Should I?' she replied with undisguised hostility.

He never seemed to notice. He waved aside the offer with a nonchalant, casual gesture and strolled away, the blue heeler bitch at his heels. Kaarin saw him flinging food to the chickens, and a few minutes later he walked into the kitchen and doled out the cattle dog's meal in a plastic bowl which he took back out on the porch with him.

A few minutes later he returned inside the cabin, replaced the pipe and tobacco in their places, and seated himself at the now-clean kitchen table with Kaarin's tape recorder before him.

He inserted a fresh tape, checked the settings on the machine, and with neither word nor glance to Kaarin, began.

'Chapter six,' he said, and began relating the story without the slightest sign of hesitation, no requirement to even check where he'd left off during his last dictation session.

Kaarin sat on the day-bed, fascinated. The voice was the one she so vividly remembered from the night before, a voice that gradually became more and more charged with passion, emotion, life ... the story and its characters seemed to move like shadows into the dimly lit room, and it was half an hour before she realised that both she and Jackson Collier were now sitting in almost total darkness.

I might as well not be here at all, she thought, sitting, a shadow among shadows as he reached the end of one side of tape, turned the cassette over, and began again without enough of a pause to break the vivid mental scenario he was creating.

The first tape complete, he halted only long enough

to walk over to the fridge, open a can of beer, and change cassettes. Then it began all over again, and Kaarin sat unmoving throughout. Never in her life had she encountered such a story-teller, and she was admittedly mesmerised.

As his voice moved into the next tape and the next chapter, Kaarin closed her eyes and sprawled out comfortably on the bed with her head supported by pillows. Lying in the darkness, her ears totally attuned to Jackson Collier's narrative, she let herself become completely immersed in the story, and after a time she began to drift right into the heroine's character, living and experiencing the terrors, the fears, and the love that the author had given his heroine to carry in a torment of passion and heartbreak.

And somewhere during it all, she slid away into sleep, a deep, restful slumber that lasted into the dawn serenade from the chook pen. No nightmares, only a vague uncertainty about the difference between sleep and wakefulness. There was a tender half-memory of being tucked in and kissed ever so gently goodnight on the forehead, but in the light of dawn Kaarin couldn't be certain if it had actually happened or if it was something from the book.

What *was* surprising was to open her eyes and find Jackson Collier, head slumped on his forearms, sound asleep at the table. She slid quietly from the daybed, padding across the rough plank floor in her bare feet towards the bathroom. Hair brushed and shiny, her teeth cleaned and a fresh application of sunburn cream on the now-fading angry redness, she returned to the kitchen to find him still dead to the world.

He came awake some time during her preparation of a breakfast that was virtually identical to the tea of the night before. Steak, eggs and damper were all cooking nicely when something brought Kaarin around to find Jackson Collier watching her, a mild curiosity in his dark eyes.

'Morning,' he said with a wry grin. 'Coffee on yet?'

'It will be by the time you've washed up,' Kaarin replied, and turned back to her work as he padded off towards the bathroom. He returned and sat in silence over his coffee as she finished the meal and dished it out, then began eating with no sign that he considered conversation a significant part of breakfast. It was left to Kaarin to raise the matter of a shopping trip.

'Tomorrow, maybe. Or the next day,' was his solemn reply. 'No time today.'

'So it's steak and eggs and steak and eggs for ever,' Kaarin replied half-angrily. 'Don't you get sick of it?'

'Ummm . . .' He shrugged and lapsed back into silence.

'Well, I'm sick of it already,' she snapped. 'And I'm going to town for some decent, civilised food whether you like it or not.'

He looked up at her, eyes slightly crinkled with what might have been a tolerant amusement. 'I'd rather you started on the typing,' he said quietly, and there was a rigidity in his voice that warned her against opposing him.

She ignored the warning, her anger spilling over as she shouted at him.

'Oh, damn the typing! You may be some kind of human machine, but I'm not and I don't intend to be. If you want to subsist on such a . . . boring, monotonous diet, that's your privilege, but you can't expect me to do it!'

He merely raised one eyebrow mockingly as he stood up from the table, plucked the T-bones from his plate and Kaarin's, and walked to the door. Whistling up the dog, he presented her with the bones, then sauntered over to her camper, returning a moment later with the big typewriter cradled in his arms.

He placed it on the table, then without a word

gathered his T-shirt and work gloves and left the room again, this time headed for his building site.

Kaarin sat in stunned, angry silence, part of her mind urging her to shout after him, to demand some kind of confrontation, some meaningful dialogue, and the other part admitting that she'd just had her confrontation—and lost!

Fuming with frustration, she cleaned up after the meal, released the chickens from their coop and then angrily stalked out to the camper, where she rummaged through her wardrobe for a fresh blouse and jeans.

The nerve of the man! Ten minutes under the shower and a fresh cup of coffee did nothing to improve her temperament, nor did the looming spectre of the typewriter, which squatted like some malevolent idol on the kitchen table.

Finally she could stand it no more. Grabbing up her handbag and—as a last-minute thought—the hat Jackson Collier had brought her, she slammed out of the house and over to her van. The typing could wait, she thought, if for no other reason than to spite the obnoxious Jackson Collier.

It took her only a few minutes to batter down the various loose gear in the back of the van, and by the time she'd got ready to leave, her mind was already filling with visions of fat cheeseburgers, loaded with pickles and beetroot and lettuce and salad. And fresh bread, and milk, and ...

'That's strange,' she muttered aloud, then turned to rummage through her handbag. The van keys weren't there either, and her eyes turned again to the empty ignition.

Puzzled, certain she'd simply left the keys in the ignition on her arrival, she walked slowly back to the house and spent several minutes rummaging through her other clothes, then her travel case, and finally the kitchen itself. Realisation came slowly, not least because her suspicions seemed so incredibly unbelievable.

'Rotten swine! Oh, you wouldn't dare. You ... couldn't!'

But as she slammed the hat on her head and walked angrily to the brow of the ridge, Kaarin knew deep inside that he would dare—and he had!

The look in his eye as she strode down to stand in front of him confirmed her suspicions, as did the slight twisting of his generous mouth as he paused in his work and straightened at her approach.

'Finished already?' The intonation of the two words revealed the laughter inside him, and served only to fuel the fires of rage within her.

She glared up at him, one hand outstretched. 'My keys, if you don't mind.'

He didn't answer at first, but put on an almost convincing exhibition of puzzlement. And then, 'What keys?'

'You know damned well what keys,' she retorted. 'The keys to my van, of course. It's the only thing around here that's worth locking up, although I'm beginning to think that *you* ought to be!'

'But your van isn't locked.' His reply was mild, not provocative except for the unholy gleam in his eyes as he met her gaze squarely.

'Give ... me ... the keys,' Kaarin grated. 'Now!'

'Why?'

The blunt reply startled her slightly, as it was clearly meant to do. 'Because ... because I want them,' she snapped back.

'Why?'

'Because I want to go and buy some decent food, that's why!' she almost screamed, barely restraining the urge to strike out at him with her fists, or kick him, or ... something.

'Oh,' he said. 'We'll go tomorrow, maybe.' There

was dismissal in his tone, confirmed as he bent down to pick up his shovel once again.

Kaarin reacted so quickly she surprised even herself, and certainly she surprised Jack Collier when she slammed one foot down on the shovel before he could lift it.

'Now,' she said firmly. 'I want to go now!' And as his eyes moved from her face to the shovel and back again, she demanded, 'Now give me the keys.'

'I don't have your keys,' he said then, and she could have screamed.

'Of course you've got them,' she cried. 'And you know it, too. Now are you going to hand them over, or . . .' Words failed her then, as much from her anger as anything else.

'Or . . . what?' he grinned. And then, surprisingly, he folded his arms across his chest and regarded her insolently. 'Search me, if it'll make you any happier.'

'I doubt it,' Kaarin replied hotly, then flushed at the ridiculousness of his suggestion as her eyes moved down across the broad, muscular chest to the only place her keys could conceivably be, in his shorts.

His shorts! Faded, denim cut-offs that fitted his lean figure like a second skin, revealing in their tightness almost as much as they concealed. Every contour of his hips and groin was in bold relief as her eyes flashed over him, touching on the obviously empty pockets, the taut, muscular seat and the flatness of the stomach. But there were no keys hidden there; in fact, virtually nothing was hidden, and well he knew it.

'Hardly what I'd call a thorough search,' he chuckled as Kaarin stepped back in embarrassed confusion, her eyes averted from his mocking gaze. And as she turned and fled back up the hill, stumbling in her haste and mortification, the sound of his laughter echoed in her ears.

Once out of his sight, however, her anger boiled over

in a flood of frustrated tears, and she had to pause, leaning against the side of his old utility, until she could once again see clearly. Beside her, the cattle dog bitch whuffled into her trembling fingers, and she leaned down to scratch at its ears.

As she straightened up, a flash of reflected sunlight from inside the utility caught her eye, and she turned with a cry of delight to find that Jackson Collier's keys, at least, were accessible to her.

'And serve you right as well,' she muttered angrily, trotting back to the cabin for her purse. The dog, trotting along beside her, threw up its head as if in agreement, but when Kaarin reached the utility again and reached for the door handle, the dog's attitude suddenly changed entirely.

A low, anxious growl was her first indication, and she paused to look down, surprised more than anything else. But as she reached again to open the door, the growl deepened, ominous now, and she pulled back her hand.

'Oh, come now,' she said soothingly. 'It's all right, you know me now, don't you?'

The only reply was another growl that deepened as she attempted to reach down and placate the bitch.

She retreated a few steps, hoping the dog would come with her, and it did, but always moving cautiously, its suspicions aroused and the instinct to guard roused past any memory of Kaarin's friendliness.

The following ten minutes were an exercise in frustration almost as bad as anything Jackson Collier himself might provide. The dog had made up its mind, and nothing Kaarin could do or say would change that. When she returned to the house, the animal trotted with her, and inside the building was as friendly as one might expect. Until she tried to collar it, which brought a low growl of warning, and when she tried for the second and third times to get into Jack Collier's truck, then the warnings were even more ominous.

Finally she had to give it up, knowing only too well the folly of an open conflict she could only lose. There was simply no way to argue with jaws that could crush her wrists like toothpicks, and a loyalty she couldn't honestly condemn.

Eventually she returned to the cabin for good, stopping to collect a ream of typing paper from the van on her way. She would find some way to get even, but just at the moment she had absolutely no idea how she'd manage it. And much as it irked her, the typing *would* have to be done eventually, so it might as well begin now.

It was ludicrous, she thought a moment later, when she sat down and placed the dictaphone headset over her ears and found the blue heeler bitch snuggling against her feet so firmly it threatened the operation of the foot control.

'Now that is going just too far!' she cried angrily, and flung off the headphones as she rose and ordered the dog outside. 'And damned well stay outside!' she shouted, slamming the door and stamping back to start her work anew.

But once she started, the pace of the book quickly caught her up, and she quickly found herself becoming as immersed in the story as she had on the evening previous. Not having heard the first chapters, she found the exercise even more fascinating, and her fingers flew over the keyboard as page after page of the first draft was typed.

She was so engrossed that she never thought again of her stalemate with the dog, or even of her aborted mission to collect more supplies. She was typing swiftly and with total concentration when instinct warned her of Jack Collier's return.

She paused only long enough to glare up at him, eyes cold with a contempt that curled up her lip into a deliberate sneer, then she turned back to the typewriter, pointedly ignoring her host and employer.

But it was a façade she couldn't maintain; once knowing he was in the room with her she found his presence pervading her thoughts, and finally she stopped typing with the knowledge that if she didn't pause she'd end up making mistakes through her lack of concentration.

Once she'd stopped, pulling away the headphones and shaking her hair away as she became aware of her stiffness from sitting so long, Jack Collier stepped forward and picked up the last page on the growing stack at her right.

Kaarin sat in silence as he surveyed the work, seeming to read the entire page word by word before he replaced it exactly as he'd found it.

'Good,' he said. 'What's for lunch?'

'Anything you feel like cooking,' she replied coldly, fighting to maintain control. His lack of any compliment on her work didn't upset her greatly; she'd have been surprised if he had commented. But his obvious assumption that she'd be cook and cleaning lady as well as typist was too much to bear gracefully. If there was going to be a fight over it, and she fully expected one, it might as well be now.

'Umm,' he said quite noncommittally, and to her surprise turned away without another word and began sorting kindling into the ancient wood stove. The fire lit, he strode over to commandeer a can of beer from the fridge and wandered out to sit on the porch while he drank it. There was no move, of course, to think of offering one to Kaarin—not that she'd have accepted anyway.

Angrily, she returned to her typing, stabbing at the keys with quick, brittle movements and determined to ignore the rudeness and frustration of Collier.

He wandered back in a few minutes later, and Kaarin did her best to ignore him as he slid into the all-too-familiar routine of steaks on the griddle and eggs in the pan. It was all she could do to hold her stomach down at the smell of the searing meat.

'How do you want your steak?'

The question startled her, especially as he'd been forced to raise his voice to counter the speech from the dictaphone, and Kaarin threw her head around in alarm. Then she found the gist of the question and made a distasteful grimace.

'Not for me. I simply couldn't face it,' she replied coldly. 'In fact I don't think I could even stand to watch you eat it.'

Tugging aside the headphones, she was halfway to the door when he halted her by closing one strong hand around her left arm.

'You've got to eat,' he said firmly. 'Working on an empty stomach is bad for you. Ruin your disposition.'

Kaarin stared into his dark eyes, searching for the mockery she knew would be there somewhere.

'My disposition is my own business,' she countered, struggling vainly to free herself. 'If you want me to eat, then give me back my car keys so that I can go and buy something decent.'

'Nothing the matter with steak and eggs,' he replied, easily turning her around and firmly seating her at the table. 'Besides, think of all the starving millions in Asia.'

Under any other circumstances, she might have laughed at his use of the ancient line, but now it served only to make her more angry.

'You think of them!' she cried, erupting from the chair. She managed half a step before he reached out to capture her once more.

'You'll do as you're told,' he told her savagely, thrusting her back into the chair.

'I won't!'

'You damn well will, if I have to tie you into the

chair and force-feed you.' His eyes revealed it to be a serious threat.

'What kind of monster are you?' Kaarin cried. 'My God! Do you really imagine for one minute that you can . . . order me around as if this was some kind of jail?'

'Certainly,' he replied without a hint of smile. 'Don't forget it wasn't my idea for you to be here. Blame your boss for that. And while you're here you'll do things my way, or I'll raise such a stink with Bill Cleaver that you'll be in strife for ever.'

Kaarin snorted angrily. She certainly wasn't going to reveal to this . . . this animal, that Bill Cleaver would be more than ready to give his 'niece' a fair hearing should Jackson Collier decide to complain.

'All he could do is fire me, which would be a great relief under the circumstances,' she countered.

'Not until the book's done,' he replied. 'Now are you going to sit there and eat your lunch like a good little girl, or do I have to tie you down?'

'Oh, all right. I'll eat your damned steak,' Kaarin snapped.

'Good!' He returned to the stove and dished up the meal, then sat down across from Kaarin and stared at her until she began to eat.

Every single mouthful was a struggle, but under Jack Collier's fierce gaze Kaarin did as well as she could, and ended up by eating almost half the enormous steak he'd cooked for her. He seemed under no such handicap; he demolished his own steak, four eggs, and after shooting Kaarin a look of frank disgust, reached over and shovelled the remains of her steak on to his own plate. He ate it, too, somewhat to her surprise.

'Not much wonder you're so skinny,' he grunted when his meal was done. 'You should eat more.'

'I'm hardly what any sane person would consider skinny,' Kaarin retorted. 'And if you'd get some decent tucker in this . . . this concentration camp, I'd have no trouble eating my share. Now if you don't mind, I'd like to get back to my work, so why don't you go play with your shovel or something.'

'Temper, temper,' he smirked. 'You'll give yourself ulcers, and that wouldn't do at all.' And then, with a positively wicked grin, 'If I did get you something besides steak for tea tonight, could you cook it on that old wood stove?'

'Well, of course I could,' Kaarin replied hotly. 'Better than you, at any rate, although it wouldn't take much.'

'Right,' he said, and rising lithely to his feet, he strode out the door, returning a minute later with a squawking hen under his arm.

'How about this, then?' he asked, and every aspect of his demeanour suggested to Kaarin that he quite expected her to shriek and run for cover.

'If you insist,' she replied calmly, reaching out to take the outraged hen from him. 'But personally I'd think it would make more sense to kill one of the cockerels you've got running around out there. Or don't you care about keeping up the supply of eggs to go with your steak?'

Her answer was a grin that slowly spread across his face, revealing broad white teeth and a wealth of laugh lines she'd never noticed before. 'Score one for you,' he said, bowing almost graciously before her. 'Okay, take this one back and exchange it, and you can spend the afternoon making us a non-boring dinner while I see if I can't finish off the book.'

'With pleasure!' Kaarin snapped, her elation almost too much to bear. She'd show him! It was plain as the nose on his face that he expected her to cry for help in killing and cleaning the chicken, but for once Mr Jackson Collier was going to be shown up for the chauvinistic twit that he was.

Pausing only long enough to grab up the kitchen carving knife, she plunged through the door and off to the chicken run, where she exchanged the hen for not one but two young cockerels, noting for future reference that there were still three left.

It was while she was casting about for a suitable site to deal with the chickens that her eye chanced upon a flash of green foliage that seemed much too bright, lacking the characteristic dull, almost grey-green colouration of the scrub.

Inspection provided Kaarin with a surge of unexpected delight—it was a garden. Abandoned, neglected and horribly overgrown, but a garden nevertheless. And even better, it contained useable quantities of peas, beans, and even—incredibly—some potatoes.

How fantastic, she thought, then experienced a brief surge of anger towards Jackson Collier. Surely, she reckoned, he must have known the garden existed? But then maybe not? he seemed so totally immersed in his house-building that perhaps he hadn't even bothered to explore the surroundings.

And when she finally returned to the house, two carefully plucked and dressed chickens in hand, it was to find Jackson Collier staring with vacant eyes across the top of the recorder as his voice surged ahead with his story. She couldn't help but admire the man's abilities, especially the blinkered concentration he was able to effect. Working in a kitchen she'd yet to fully explore, Kaarin couldn't help but make a fair bit of noise as she rummaged about in search of a suitable roasting pan and various other implements, yet Collier continued to dictate as if he were alone in the room.

He seemed not to notice her existence as Kaarin prepared the chickens, built up the fire in the stove, walked down to the building site for a shovel to dig up the potatoes and—after getting the evening meal under way—set about the necessary housekeeping jobs.

But if Jack Collier could ignore her, Kaarin certainly couldn't do the same for him. His voice followed her as she moved through the house, and she found herself pausing more and more often to simply listen as the closing chapters of his book unfolded.

The first time he paused to change tapes and collect a chilled can of beer, she was busy sweeping the porch, but the second time she was standing beside the fridge, listening, and when he paused, she quietly took out a fresh beer, opened it, and placed it near his hand. The gesture, done without conscious expectation of a response, gained Kaarin a quick, darting look of surprise that momentarily cleared away the far-off, lost look in his dark eyes.

Then he nodded, a curt, abrupt gesture of acceptance, and his eyes seemed to fade away again immediately as his voice once again picked up the tale.

He started on the final chapter at five o'clock, and Kaarin, by that time, had given up any semblance of ignoring him. She sat crosslegged on the narrow day bed, her eyes closed as she allowed the words to flow in and around her, thrilling to the climax of the tale as it emerged from the writer's lips.

The climax was startling, almost graphic in its sensuality and brutal impact, but the dénouement was far more subtle, being more erotic than roughly sensuous, bringing out every thread of emotion. Just listening to it made Kaarin unaccountably aware of her own femininity, of the rising tides of passion in her slender body. She could feel herself responding to the emotions in the story, no longer consciously hearing the words, but feeling, living them. The warmth that flowed to a gentle stirring in the pit of her stomach seemed to spread then throughout her body, making her feel almost as if she were suspended, floating wraithlike above the reality of the world around her.

Waves of sensation gently rocked her; she was the

book's heroine, riding a whirlwind of passion that built and grew and surrounded her. And when the hero, a faceless, mystic figure, touched her, readying her for the final surrender, Kaarin felt her body responding, her fingers reaching out to touch him, her lips moving to meet his, her eyes opening to look into his own dark, passionate eyes.

And suddenly her eyes flew open as reality touched her, exploding the dream. The eyes she'd seen, the face had suddenly taken on an identity, and she was shocked by the physical impact of it. It was as if Jackson Collier had physically moved into her fantasy, yet he hadn't moved; he still sat, silent now, staring over the tape recorder with brooding, distant eyes.

And yet he remained in her mind as well, a figure so distinctly sexual, so masculine, and so tuned to her emotions that Kaarin shivered slightly at the thought of it.

The impact was so jolting she shook her head as if to whisk it away. But it could not, would not simply disappear. When she closed her eyes again, she found her mind drinking in the lust in his eyes, then shifting dreamlike to the memory of his naked body on the river rocks.

Never in her life had any man had such a physical impact on her, and never indeed with so little and so unlikely an effort. Jackson Collier had never so much as looked at her as a woman, and his responses to her had been in no way sexual, but Kaarin now found herself attracted in a way she couldn't even totally comprehend. It would have been ludicrous had it not been so completely, gut-wrenchingly real.

The realisation churned up an immediate typhoon of panic inside her; she couldn't stay here now, couldn't possibly remain—alone in the bush—with a man who had so vividly stirred her physical and emotional responses without even trying. Suppose he did, now that the book was finished, begin to notice Kaarin as the attractive woman she knew herself to be? Could she possibly resist him? Gone was the earlier anger, the frustration, the coldness. Now she looked at Jack Collier through different eyes, and was frightened by the sheer strength of her reactions.

'Hey ... come back!' The voice brought her suddenly wide-eyed to reality as she looked up to find Jack Collier standing over her, his dark eyes alive and vibrant as he looked down with apparent concern.

'I didn't mean to startle you,' he said with unexpected gentleness, 'but you looked as if wherever you were it wasn't the right place.'

'It ... wasn't, I guess,' she replied uncertainly. Surely he could see in her eyes the very thing she so desperately wanted to avoid, the new awareness of him as a handsome, exceptionally desirable man.

'What's the matter—the book turn you on a bit?' There was a hint of the old mockery in his eyes now, a bold, piratical assessment that Kaarin shrunk from unconsciously.

'Of course ... n-not!' She floundered over the reply, striving for boldness and knowing she failed. Her body betrayed her; she knew her breasts were taut with the impact of him, her loins suddenly warm and alive.

'You're lying,' he said flatly. 'You'd better be, anyway, or I'm in all kinds of trouble, because it was supposed to be erotic as hell.'

'I'm ... sure it would be, to most women,' Kaarin replied, forcing calmness into her voice and she deliberately met his eyes.

'But not to you, eh?' He didn't expect a reply, but shook his head with silent laughter as he turned away. He clearly didn't believe her, but at least he hadn't sensed that it was he, as much as the book, who affected her.

'My word, but I'm hungry,' he said in an abrupt

change of subject that surprised Kaarin. 'When'll tea be ready?'

The chickens! Kaarin leaped from the bed as if she'd been stung. In her trance-like immersion in the climax of the book, she'd forgotten entirely about the roasting fowls. And in a wood-fired stove!

She opened the oven expecting total disaster, but a glance assured her that her fears were groundless. She'd laid the fire expertly and the stove had worked exactly as she'd planned. The two birds, plump and succulent, were nearly done, and would be ready just when she had the potatoes and vegetables ready.

'Say ... half an hour,' she replied after a quick calculation, her mind already occupied with finalising the dinner.

'Great! Leaves me just enough time for a swim,' he replied, stretching and swivelling his muscular shoulders as if to relieve a great stiffness. Which, Kaarin thought, he very likely felt after hours unmoving before the tape recorder.

The dog loped into place at Jack's heels as he strode across the yard and disappeared down the hillside to the river, and Kaarin found herself almost immediately fraught with mental visions of him standing naked on his rock, slicing through the air like a bronzed arrow when he dived into the cool, refreshing water. It was a vision that persisted as she stoked the fire and began slicing up the vegetables.

CHAPTER FOUR

JACKSON COLLIER returned exactly on time, his dark hair still damp from his swim and the play of his muscles evident beneath the still-damp T-shirt he'd obviously used as a towel.

He breathed a sigh of undisguised appreciation when Kaarin laid out the chickens on the table and set before each of them a plate piled high with potatoes, green vegetables and finally a bowl of thick chicken gravy.

The meal was delicious, amazingly so, Kaarin thought, although forced to fight down a wish for jelly of some kind to complement the flavour of the meat.

Jackson Collier had no such problems. He ate with obvious relish, but slowly, savouring every mouthful. The mountain of potatoes on his plate was drowned in gravy, and he dipped into it with a slow, almost sensuous deliberateness.

But perhaps the biggest surprise was when he reached those portions of the bird best eaten in the fingers, and politely asked Kaarin's permission before doing so.

'Of . . . of course,' she replied, surprised by the small courtesy. Added to his solemn appreciation of the meal, especially compared to the way he'd systematically demolished his steak and eggs as if fuelling a fire, it was all suddenly quite confusing.

Despite the rugged dress, the man who now shared table with her evinced all the mannerisms of a proper gentleman, even to holding her chair when she returned from getting more vegetables from the stove top.

'Fantastic! Absolutely fantastic,' he breathed when he finally settled back after finishing the meal. 'You're a blessing upon the house, Kaarin Amos, although I'm glad you didn't get here earlier.'

'I . . . don't understand what you mean,' she replied. 'Was that some kind of backhanded compliment?'

He laughed, a surprisingly genuine laugh that revealed once more the wealth of humour in his face. 'You could say that,' he replied. 'What I meant was that if I'd had cooking like that to look forward to while I was putting the book together, I'd have been so distracted by my stomach that it would have been hell on the work.'

'You've still lost me,' she was forced to say after a minute spent silently evaluating his comment.

'Hah! Now I can admit to you that steak and eggs is indeed boring! Even the rather ingenious approach you took the other day couldn't help much, if you don't mind me saying so. But I've found that when I'm writing my books, the final putting them together in my head, that is, I work much better when I can concentrate only on what I'm doing. And since I love good tucker—like, I should be twenty stone and growing—I write better when there are no choices to be made and therefore nothing to distract me. If you'd been here during that stage, I'd have spent half my time wondering what miracles you were creating in the kitchen.'

'I see . . . I think,' Kaarin replied. He did make sense in a rather weird fashion. 'Does that mean, then, that tomorrow I can really go food shopping—or does your principle extend to this house-building project as well?'

'Lord no! In fact, my lovely miracle-worker, we shall *both* take tomorrow off and spend it in an orgy of shopping. We'll drive into Bundaberg and buy out every delicacy in every supermarket in the place. *And* I'll take you for lunch in any restaurant you choose, despite the fact that I'd sell my soul for Chinese-style roast duck.'

He paused then, staring intently across the table to where Kaarin was silent with the overwhelming confusion of it all. Could this be the same arrogant, appallingly brusque, chauvinist she'd been dealing with ever since her arrival? Stealer of car keys, a man who hadn't even so much as asked her . . .?

'How do you know my name?' The question popped out even as she thought it. He had never asked her name, had never evinced any interest in knowing it, and yet . . .

He shrugged, a slight smile flickering across his face. 'I looked in your handbag, of course. When you were laid low with sunstroke that first night and I was damned near ready to take you into hospital. I reckoned they'd want to know who you were if that happened, so I looked.'

'Well, thank you very much!' Kaarin replied, flushed with an unexpected surge of anger. 'And I suppose it was then that you stole my keys, as well?'

'I did not!' But he was lying and made no attempt to hide the fact. If anything, in fact, he was clearly amused by it all.

Kaarin didn't bother to argue. She did, however, insist on having the keys returned to her. The request drew only a mildly contemptuous grin.

'What are you planning to do, run away off to Sydney at the crack of dawn?' he said then. 'I thought the book was getting to you; I could see it in your eyes. Let me guess, dear Kaarin. You're going to lock yourself into that broiling tin can of a camper tonight and spend the whole time wondering when I'm going to come and ravish you.'

'Don't be ridiculous,' Kaarin snapped. 'It's just that . . . well . . . I'd feel more comfortable there, that's all.'

One eyebrow cocked in arrogant mockery. 'You mean you haven't been comfortable the last two nights? Or hasn't it occurred to you that if I was going to take a hack at you I've had more than enough opportunity already.'

'Somehow I don't think you'd be greatly attracted by burnt offerings,' she replied, deliberately striving to keep her reply light. The reply was all right, but her involuntary response to his deliberate visual assessment of her sunburnt areas was too revealing for comfort.

'Offerings? Well, that's an angle I hadn't considered,' he said reflectively. And his eyes continued their deliberate assault on her, stripping her until she stood naked and vulnerable as a slave on the auction block. 'My very word,' he said, voice so low it was almost a whisper. 'I must have been properly into that book to have not noticed an offer like that.'

And then he grinned hugely, his amusement at Kaarin's discomfort flowing like a tide to wipe away the hot sensuality of his earlier assessment.

'Settle down ... settle down. I'm Jack the writer, not Jack the Ripper. Besides, after today's performance, I'd have to be mad to risk losing such a cook just for a moment's uncontrolled lust.'

'And besides, the book isn't typed yet,' Kaarin replied, rising to meet the humour in his eyes. Even at his worst, she hadn't reckoned him for a mauler, and despite her growing confusion at his mercurial mood changes, she knew instinctively she was in no danger at all from Jackson Collier. The danger was within herself, in the growing awareness she had of him as a man she could too easily lose her head over.

'Right!' he replied with a devastating grin. 'But the typing can wait until after tomorrow's gastronomic adventure.'

He literally flung himself to his feet then, and glided over to collect the dirty dishes from the table.

'And now I shall clean up while you start preparing your shopping list,' he said cheerfully. 'With appropriate consultation, of course, unless you'd rather just take the place by storm and see what delicacies are available?'

'I think we'd better have some sort of list,' she agreed, 'and really, I'll do the dishes. You've put in a terribly hard day's work already, and I've only . . .'

'Only created miracles,' he grinned. 'No way; save your lovely hands for the typewriter, dear girl. I'm not afraid of a little soap and water. Just get out your notebook and we'll see how close our tastes are when it comes to food.'

By the time the dishes were done, Kaarin had a list that resembled a stock-list for Sydney's finest delicatessen. And she found that Jackson Collier's sense of humour extended itself in strange areas indeed.

'First—no steak. No eggs.' He'd insisted that she head the list with that, and periodically inserted it into the mammoth shopping list he dictated as he methodically washed the dishes. It was surprising to find how closely their tastes in food emerged, also. Throughout the list, he insisted upon Kaarin's right to veto what she didn't fancy, not that it mattered a great deal. If they bought everything on the list, she reckoned, it would take a semi-trailer to bring it all home again. Home . . . she shivered a touch at the thought.

It seemed incredible, considering the trauma of the past few days, for Kaarin to even remotely think of this isolated, run-down cabin as home. But with Jackson Collier's sudden transition from a conceited, arrogant sod to a charming, comfortable companion, it seemed that the quiet and peace of the setting had flowed in to soothe Kaarin's jangled nerves.

She, too, looked forward with excitement to the next day's shopping expedition, and as the evening progressed she found Jack's enthusiasm highly contagious. He brought out the drawings of his housing project, and his facility with words brought the concept into a visual, living thing for her.

She could suddenly understand his desire to build his house himself, using the ancient traditional methods of post-and-beam combined with adobe bricks—bricks he would make himself from the earth of his own land, timbers he would hew himself from his own trees.

'Mind you, it may turn out to be a magnificent folly,' he said at one point. 'I've never so much as thought of trying anything like this before, so I'll probably muck something up terribly before I'm done. But I don't care; even if the thing doesn't end up perfect—which it won't—the satisfaction is absolutely amazing.'

The foundations, he said, were 'near as dammit to done', and his timbers were already cut and ready. All that remained now was to get the post-and-beam framing up and he was ready for the real work—the bricks.

'It'll be a lot of hard work, but I'm really looking forward to it,' he said. And then, with a wry grin, 'and with you doing the cooking, at least I know I'll be fed up enough to stand the strain.'

Kaarin felt herself warm with the compliment, though she only smiled in response. It was going to be next to impossible, she thought, to keep up to his impression of her culinary abilities, but perhaps if he worked hard enough on his house he'd be too hungry to notice the occasional failure she knew must occur.

'Come on, I'll walk you back to your sardine can,' he said then, unexpectedly. 'We'll be getting an early start and you can probably use the rest.'

It made a difficult moment for Kaarin, who'd forgotten entirely her earlier need to escape to the sanctuary of her camper. Now, faced with the decision already made, she could only fall in with Jack's suggestion, so she collected her toiletries and walked out with him into the brilliance of a moonlit night so clear it was barely dark.

The pressure of his fingers against her own was somehow comforting, reassuring, but at the same time a throbbing reminder of her awareness of him. He was silent as they walked the short distance, but Kaarin could sense that he, too, had become subtly aware of the distinct change in their relationship.

He didn't release her fingers when they reached the van, but used his free hand first to open the door, then to take the toilet case from her and set it just inside. Still without a word, he slowly turned Kaarin round, so that she was facing him.

Fingers reached up to flicker delicately across her temple, then down the softness of her cheek until they cupped her chin lightly, raising her face slightly to meet his descending lips. Kaarin didn't resist; as his lips moved across her own, searching, exploring, but not in any way threatening, she allowed her mouth to soften with the contact.

Then both his arms were around her, not confining but exquisitely gentle in their entrapment. His fingers moved like mist across her back, her shoulders, through the heavy softness of her hair. Her own arms gradually slid along his upper arms, over his shoulders to where her fingers could flex and mingle with the coarse thickness of his nape.

Forgotten was any criticism of his arrogance, his stoic silences, his ruthless controlling of her earlier movements. As his lips brushed like featherdown over her mouth, then up her cheek and across her forehead, Kaarin could feel only the half-remembered pleasure of a good night kiss during her sunstroke. Her own lips moved on an exploration of their own, tasting the texture of his beard, the smoothness of his cheek.

As his fingers traced patterns of ecstasy along her spine, Kaarin could feel her breasts hardened by the pressure and heat and intense nearness of his chest. Her fingers tangled in his hair, tugging almost of their own volition to bring her closer yet against him.

Then his hands shifted lower, closing around her buttocks as he pulled her closer, so close that she felt the firmness of his masculinity against her soft, melting tummy. His knee was moving, sliding between her legs as he held her moulded to him, his fingers promising unspoken delight . . . his lips promising heaven without saying a word.

When his posture shifted, easing the pressure between them as his hand slipped round to move up the flatness of her stomach, then cupping each of her breasts in turn, her instinctive withdrawal was throttled by the cradle of his other arm around her, by the track of fire his lips laid as they moved down her cheek, her throat, into the hotness of the sunburn between her breasts.

His hands moved, shifting lower along her body to touch at the most sensitive, most reactive places, and her back arched with her physical need of him.

And then, his breath ragged with his own obvious desires, he pulled his lips away long enough to mutter, 'The hell with this—let's go back to the cabin.'

Before Kaarin could even think to answer, he'd lifted her into his arms, cradling her like a baby but holding her as much with his lips as his hands.

But the spell had been broken by his words, and her mind slid back from its hermitage in the land of desires, slid back and screamed.

'No! Oh, no, I can't!' she cried softly, writhing to free her mouth, then harder to try and free the body that still threatened to betray her.

Jack, still moving towards the cabin, took several steps more, his lips searching for Kaarin's mouth, seeking to once again assure his mastery, but it was too late.

With the freeing of her voice had come the release of her conscience, and she knew that she dared not succumb to the blind dictates of her passion-ripened body.

'Put me down,' she cried. 'Oh, please put me *down*!' And then, with a sob, 'I can't ... I simply can't!'

He paused, and then with a grunt of acceptance he slowly lowered her to let her feet touch the ground. They arrived already moving, and Kaarin spun herself from his arms and fled to her camper, her breath coming in short, ragged gasps as she flung open the door and dived into the sanctuary of the darkened interior.

When she looked up a minute later, Jack remained a statue in the moonlight, his eyes burning as he stared back towards her. Then he looked away, his gaze stretching down towards the river bank and the softly-tinkling waters of his pool. As he moved, then, plunging down the bank like a wraith of the night, Kaarin's control dissolved in a flood of unexplainable tears.

The remainder of the night seemed to pass in the blinking of an eye, and when she peered sleepily out of the van window at piccaninny dawn, it was to see the figure of Jack Collier gliding smoothly up the hillside, water from his morning swim gleaming in droplets on his skin. He wore only a pair of cut-off shorts and his sandals, and in the early light she couldn't see the look in his eyes.

It was easier a moment later when he thundered upon the camper-van with his fist and shouted, 'Breakfast in twenty minutes, and it's steak and eggs whether you like it or not. We haven't got anything else.'

He was gone before Kaarin could get the van door opened, and as he marched towards his cabin with the blue heeler at his side, he didn't once look back.

Kaarin debated her own moves. She wasn't going anywhere without a shower, or at least a swim, and she decided a shower was preferable. She was mildly uncertain about facing Jack, but it would have to happen sooner or later, so why not sooner? In the cold light of dawn she knew only too well that any blame for the incident of the night before was as much her own as his, perhaps more so. Indeed, if anything she was more upset at having let it start than at having had to stop the proceedings in such an undignified fashion.

His grin of welcome when she reached the cabin certainly indicated no hard feelings on his part, and he didn't bring up the matter until they'd both struggled through a breakfast that neither really enjoyed.

'Well, thank goodness this is the last of it for a while,' he said quietly then, and leaned back in his chair with a grateful sigh. 'Promise, Kaarin—no more steak and eggs until at least Christmas next year.'

'I rather doubt that I'll be here that long,' she murmured shyly. 'I can't imagine me needing longer than a fortnight to type your book.'

'And after last night you're worried that it might be three weeks too long at that,' he grinned wryly. 'Well, don't! I promise here and now to keep my hands to myself—except if I catch you outside without your hat.'

'That isn't what I was thinking at all,' Kaarin replied. Which wasn't much of a lie. She was more worried about her own reactions to Jack's advances than about whether he'd make any or not. She was silent for a moment, but he didn't respond. 'Do I really have to wear that silly hat into town today?' she asked.

'Not if you don't want to,' he shrugged. And then, with a rather boyish grin, 'I don't think it would go with your outfit, now that you mention it. Very nice, if I may say so.'

'Thank you,' she smiled, and was inordinately pleased that he'd noticed, even knowing that the pale blue halter-necked sundress was extremely flattering to her. The ravages of the sunburn had now faded to leave only a slight darkening in her cleavage, but she'd been careful to apply liberal quantities of sunscreen after finishing her shower.

Jack's choice of route into Bundaberg wasn't exactly the one Kaarin would have chosen, especially since it didn't even exist on the motoring club map she'd studied before heading north. But it was all the more pleasant, she thought, because of its scenic attractions and the fact they didn't travel quickly.

After leaving the property, they drove across Mingo Crossing itself, now a fine, high concrete bridge which afforded views of the original, now broken wooden low-level bridge a few yards upstream. The waters of the Burnett River were clear and sparkling as they tumbled over the rocky riverbed, sliding into deep dark pools where small fish leapt at low-flying insects.

Once across the bridge, Jack steered north and then east, travelling on a narrow gravel road that crossed grazing land dotted with bright, fat cows, then narrowed to a mere track as they negotiated the Goodnight Scrub, most of which was a classified state forest.

Jack drove his elderly utility with a casual expertise, his eyes roving constantly as he pointed out first a flock of white cockatoos, then a larger, more colourful group of lorikeets that flashed like windblown opals at the vehicle's approach.

It was Kaarin, however, who first spotted the big old red-necked scrub turkey quietly dusting itself in the dirt of the roadside, and as Jack slowed at her cry of excitement, the large bird scooted for cover, then paused for a final look before disappearing into the brush.

Kaarin had long since lost all sense of direction when, after negotiating a confusing maze of bush tracks, Jack steered the utility across the Burnett River on a concrete barrage, then up a few kilometres of gravel track to rejoin the main Bruce Highway once again.

A few moments later they were at Apple Tree Creek and the junction with the Isis Highway and heading north-east into Bundaberg.

'We'll go back a different route, mostly,' Jack said at the junction. 'One without all the rough going. It's a lot faster, but you won't see anything like that turkey on the bitumen.'

'Oh, I don't mind the way we came,' Kaarin replied. 'I'd far rather travel slowly and see whatever there is to see. I'd never seen a scrub turkey before, as a matter of fact. Aren't they quite rare?'

'Increasingly,' came the almost gruff reply. 'Although there are plenty of them in the Goodnight Scrub, provided you get away from the roads. The trouble is that once their nesting mounds are discovered, it doesn't take much effort to find the birds themselves, and they're about the finest bush tucker there is.'

'That sounds like the voice of experience,' Kaarin answered, a hint of reproof obvious in her voice. She didn't consider herself an ardent conservationist, but she didn't hold with indiscriminate killing of rare wildlife.

'Not any experience I'm especially proud of,' Jack replied. 'Although at the time there wasn't the push for conservation that exists today. Nor the money either, if I may say so. You can tell by the look of the old homestead that we weren't exactly prosperous graziers or anything when I was a lad, and bush tucker was an accepted aspect of our diet. There's been a Christmas or two I can remember when scrub turkey was far more than a luxury—it was *all* there was.'

The frankness of the revelation set the tone of their

conversation as they completed the journey into Bundaberg, and when it was over Kaarin had not only found out a good deal about Jackson Collier's childhood, but had told him as much—if not more—about her own circumstances.

On the death of his parents in a car crash when he was eleven, Jack had been shifted to Sydney to be raised by a maiden aunt, and after finishing his schooling had embarked upon a journalistic career spanning much of the globe before his books began to sell enough that he could devote himself entirely to writing.

'The property was sold, oh, three or four times at least after the folks died,' he said. 'I bought it back—at a ridiculous price—when I was thirty, always with the idea of doing just what I'm doing now. But the past seven years haven't given me the time, or quite the incentive, until just recently.'

Kaarin was silent, her mind mulling over what he'd left unsaid. Incentive? Was his break-up with Neridah Gregg the incentive, she wondered, or the associated desire to flee from the socialite world in which he'd gained such prominence and prestige? Either way, it was certainly none of her business, but then why did the thought of the beautiful socialite Neridah Gregg bring such a surge of anger to her insides? She had almost decided to risk asking for more information when they passed the Hinkler Airport and entered the outskirts of the sugar city.

Jack drove immediately to the city centre, telling Kaarin as they sped along that they'd return to the Sugarland shopping centre on the outskirts to pick up their groceries as the final stop on the way home.

'Anywhere special you'd like to go?' he asked then. 'I've got a few things to do this morning; then I thought we'd have a long, leisurely lunch and then head back.'

It was clear he didn't want her with him throughout the morning, which Kaarin found slightly offputting, but it saved her the exercise of evading him long enough to telephone a detailed report to Uncle Bill, so she didn't really have any right to criticise.

'No, I'll just wander around and have a look at the place,' she said. 'I've never been here before, so I'm sure there'll be plenty to see by playing tourist.'

'Hmph! Not unless it's changed a helluva lot since I was a kid,' he replied. 'They may call it a city now, but it's really still just a big country town.'

'And what's wrong with that?' Kaarin replied hotly. It was among her pet peeves that her home town of Dubbo, which was about the same size as Bundaberg, seemed to have become the butt of incessant jokes and rude comments in various newspapers and even television programmes in New South Wales. So much so, indeed, that she'd thought herself inured to the type of scathing remarks that invariably followed her admission to having been born and raised there.

'Personally, I rather prefer country towns,' she continued, then realised she'd been caught out when she saw the quirk of amusement around Jack's mouth.

'You're being defensive,' he said with a grin. 'And I have nothing against country towns myself, dear girl. In fact I infinitely prefer them to the hassles of the city, despite the fact that they tend to be something of a cultural desert from some points of view.'

'Well, not from mine,' she snapped, more angry at having been led into the argument than at what Jack Collier was actually saying.

'Oh, settle down,' he growled in mock anger. 'Nobody's having a go at you. All I ask of the place is one decent restaurant. Give me that after what I've been eating the past month or so—your contributions excepted, of course—and I'll think it's heaven on earth and a cultural oasis to boot.'

'I'm sure it will have several,' Kaarin replied, not at all mollified by his gruffness.

'One is all I'll need,' he replied, swinging the utility into one of the all-day parking stalls off Quay Street near the bridge across the Burnett River.

They agreed then to meet again at the car at ten o'clock, provided Jack had his business completed by then, and if not, at eleven-thirty, giving them time to seek out an appropriate restaurant for lunch.

Kaarin spent the early part of the morning prowling the main shopping district, mostly window-shopping but also merely savouring the atmosphere of the bustling little city. It was, she decided, just about the right size for her; sufficiently endowed with the various shopping amenities and yet small enough that the eternal tension and rush of a large city didn't exist.

At nine-thirty she directed her strolling towards the main post office with its row of telephone booths just down the block, and registered a collect call to Bill Cleaver in Sydney.

'You're phoning to say you'll be sending the manuscript within a fortnight,' he said without preamble after accepting the call.

Kaarin was only mildly startled. 'You're reading my mind,' she replied. 'Or else . . .'

'Or else Collier phoned first,' he replied. 'Which he did. You seem to have made quite an impression, my dear. He spent nearly ten minutes of my valuable time singing your praises. Quite surprising, it was.'

'He didn't!' Now she was surprised. It seemed, if nothing else, to be quite out of character for the moody Mr Collier to even think of such a thing.

'My word! In fact he was so damned agreeable I began to worry just a bit,' Bill Cleaver replied. 'What have you been doing, putting happy pills in his food?'

'Not exactly,' she replied with a slow grin. 'In fact you wouldn't believe the trauma I went through just to get him into town today for supplies. Can you imagine what that man was living on—had been living on for, what, months before I got here? Steak and eggs and steak and eggs and steak and eggs. And beer. He has a fridge stacked from top to bottom with nothing but beer and a freezer loaded to the brim with nothing but steak . . .'

'Hang on,' he interrupted. 'I don't really care about his culinary habits at the moment. How's the book? Is it up to scratch?'

'Oh, Uncle Bill, it's . . . it's just marvellous,' she gushed unintentionally. 'By far the best thing he's ever done, I think. It's all dictated; he finished yesterday and I'll begin the typing tomorrow. If I could type as quickly as he dictates you'd have the manuscript in less than two weeks, but . . .'

'Two weeks will be sufficient. Take three if you must,' he cut in. 'And now I must go, Kaarin. I've a million things to do and the twit I moved up to replace you may need an assistant just to keep up. Get the book done and phone me when it's in the mail. 'Bye now.'

Kaarin was left with a silent telephone in her hand, but the music in her heart made up for any brusqueness on her uncle's part. So Jackson Collier had been singing her praises . . . he was pleased with her. The thought seemed to intensify the brilliance of the Queensland sunshine as she bounced cheerfully along the footpath, and it seemed as if every person she met was wearing a smile of their own.

She arrived at the utility exactly on time, waited fifteen minutes without a sign of Jack Collier, but even that couldn't shake loose the glow that surrounded her like an aura. Obviously his business had taken longer than expected, she thought, strolling off finally with a half-formed intention of putting the next hour and a half to good use by investigating the city's restaurant scene.

A pleasant young clerk at the tourist bureau was reluctant to make any specific recommendations, but suggested Kaarin look through the weekly *Drum* newspaper, which carried a full listing of restaurants in Bundaberg. 'I've got a copy here somewhere,' she said, and after a few minutes spent scrambling through various stacks of literature she managed to come up with the publication.

Kaarin took the newspaper and strolled to a shady bench in the park beside the civic centre, noticing as she walked that there was a Chinese restaurant directly across the street.

'Could have saved myself the trouble,' she muttered to herself, remembering Jack's addiction to Chinese food. Nonetheless, she scanned the restaurant columns, and immediately wished she hadn't. The mention of prawn brochette had her literally drooling at the thought.

Back to the tourist bureau, where the same helpful clerk gave her directions to the restaurant, which was in Targo Street, and five minutes later Kaarin was drooling even more as she surveyed the menu on display in the window.

She was thoughtful, though still buoyant, as she walked slowly back towards the vehicle. There must be some way she could convince Jack Collier to switch his gastronomic allegiance, but how? She thought about it all the way, but by the time she'd reached the meeting place she'd decided it just couldn't be that important anyway. Her uncle's words had so uplifted her spirits that she felt it couldn't matter where they dined, so long as Jack Collier enjoyed himself she would do the same.

It was too warm in the noonday sun to stand beside the utility waiting for Jack, so Kaarin moved into the shade of an adjoining park, perching herself on the bench of a picnic table beneath a spreading, shady tree where she could watch the broad river with its flotillas of boats and pelicans and yet still keep an eye on the designated meeting spot. He wouldn't be there for fifteen minutes anyway, she decided, and turned to another survey of the restaurant columns.

'You waiting for somebody special—or will I do?'

The words jolted Kaarin from her comfortable reverie, and she looked up with alarm that immediately changed to shocking surprise.

Before her stood a tall, lean figure with Jack Collier's voice, but that was all that remained of the man with whom she'd driven into the city.

This Jack Collier, almost resplendent in a well-cut safari suit that almost exactly matched her blue dress, was every inch the sophisticated, suave writer who stared haughtily from the dust-jacket of his books.

'Sorry I missed the first meeting,' he said. 'Things took a touch longer than I'd intended.' Then his eyes caught the paper she'd been reading, and he reached out to pluck it from her nerveless fingers.

'Ha! Luncheon calls. Have you decided where we're going?' he said, dark eyes racing as he scanned the columns.

'Well,' Kaarin said uncertainly, 'there are at least two Chinese restaurants, both quite good, I understand.'

'But you've got something else in mind,' he retorted, alert as ever to the nuances of her speech. 'Well, let's hear it—or should I guess?'

'Guess,' she replied, and then with a bravado that surprised her, 'And if you're wrong we go there. If you're right, you can choose.'

One dark eyebrow raised itself in a look of haughty assertiveness softened only by his grin.

'Not very good odds,' he muttered, then turned his full attention to the columns as Kaarin ran an appreciative eye over his startling change of appearance. She took a stirring, unexpected excitement from the possibility that this man would invest in a complete outfitting of new clothes simply to take her to lunch, then immediately discarded the thought as ludicrous. Certainly he'd done it for some other reason; he'd had business that couldn't be handled in his well-worn shorts, T-shirt and thongs.

'Where's this Il Gambero?' The question cut into her daydream and she replied instinctively, without thinking.

'Straight down this street here ... about two blocks ... You guessed!'

'I really can't imagine why women think they're so mysterious,' he replied in mock disgust. 'Do you want to drive or walk?'

'But ... you won! Don't you want to ... to eat Chinese?'

'I won. I choose. And we'll walk, provided it isn't too far,' he replied, reaching down to take her arm and lift her to her feet.

And as they strolled side by side down Targo Street, crowded now with lunchtime shoppers, Kaarin's ebullience stemmed less from the thought of the lunch ahead than from the fact that he kept her arm in his throughout the walk to the restaurant. It was a feeling of ... security ... that she'd never before experienced in such incredible magnitude.

They lunched on oysters, fat succulent prawns, barramundi in caper butter sauce and a host of other seafoods, but throughout the early part of the meal Kaarin was plagued by a feeling of strangeness. Something about Jack Collier simply didn't ring true, but she was nearly finished her main course, complete with more than adequate quantities of excellent wine, before she figured out what it was.

'I know!' she cried then, staring owlishly at him

across the table. 'Now I know!'

'Marvellous,' Jack replied with a scowl. 'And just *what* do you know?'

'You've shaved off your beard,' Kaarin replied, inwardly wondering how it should have taken her so long to notice. Even as she made the statement it seemed ridiculous that she'd been met by him in the little park, walked several blocks with him and consumed most of a meal without realising he'd shaved.

'One point out of ten for observation,' he said drily. 'I hope you proof-read better than that. And just for the record, I didn't shave it off—the barber did.'

'Oh, you know what I mean,' Kaarin replied, now embarrassed by the entire discussion. Without the beard, new clothing aside, Jack looked much less the ... brigand ... and much more the sophisticated man-of-the-world portrayed by his writings. Also, she privately admitted, much more handsome overall.

The lower portion of his face, now revealed, was only slightly paler than the strong features burned so dark by his daily work in the sun, and Kaarin thought he must have only started growing the beard when he'd moved into his remote hideaway some months before.

Throughout the remainder of the meal, she found herself unable to concentrate, having to look up on occasion—whenever Jack wasn't looking—for yet another quick assessment of his shaven countenance.

Without the beard, his strong, determined chin with a definite cleft showed itself to be as forceful as the hawk nose above. Beside his generous mouth, deep lines stretched, and it was easy to see that they were laugh lines, happy lines revealing the sense of humour she was only just beginning to appreciate.

The effect was exceptionally pleasing, though each time she closed her eyes, her mind immediately brought back the original Jack Collier, scruffy beard and piratical expression. She wasn't certain which she preferred, and found herself wondering what it would be like to be kissed by this new Jack, the smooth-cheeked one with the sardonic grin.

'Don't get to liking it too much, because I'll likely quit shaving again once we're home,' he said quietly as if reading her mind, and Kaarin shivered inside at how easily he seemed to do that.

'It's hardly any of my business,' she replied lightly. 'There's nobody but the dog to mind, and I can't imagine her complaining.'

'That's the nicest thing about dogs, they aren't demanding about such things,' he growled. And there was enough bitterness in his voice that Kaarin looked at him quizzically.

'Meaning that I am?' she asked. 'I should hardly think that a fair criticism considering what I've put up with from you during the past few days. Or do you really think it's *demanding* to object to having my car keys stolen, to be ordered about like some kind of maidservant, and told to wear my hat as if I were a child . . .'

'Which is exactly what you are, in many ways,' he interrupted. 'A very attractive and a very precocious child—also very defensive. I was *not* criticising you in any way at all. So stop being so damned defensive about everything.'

'Oh,' she said, 'then pardon me if I've upset you, sir. And may I ask to whom you *were* referring?'

He shrugged noncommittally. 'You can ask,' he replied, then lapsed into silence without any attempt to enlighten her.

Kaarin's mouth ran away with her despite a mind that screamed 'Stop!' even as she was speaking.

'So there is some truth to the rumours about you and Neridah Gregg? Funny, I wouldn't have thought it.'

His eyes turned to chips of dark brown stone and Kaarin saw the muscles of his jaw contract as he fought for control. The vividness of his anger both thrilled and frightened her, and she recoiled slightly as he leaned across the table towards her.

'I wouldn't have thought it either,' he grated through clenched teeth, his voice a fearful, deadly whisper, 'but since it interests you so much, *Miss* Amos, let's get one thing straight once and for all. My relationship with Neridah Gregg or any other woman—bar yourself—is purely, simply and totally *none* of your business.

'Any comments that I may pass about women in general are just that—in general. If you choose to take them personally that's your affair. But be certain that if I have anything to say which concerns you specifically, there will be no doubt in your mind who I mean. No doubt at all!'

'I'm ... I'm sorry,' Kaarin replied, rightly chastised. 'I ...'

'And so you should be,' he growled. 'This is supposed to be a day of gargantuan gastronomic orgies, not a day for frivolous discussions about my love life or yours, presuming you have one, or anybody else's. So concentrate on your tucker, dear Kaarin, and don't spoil it by thinking too much.'

'I was only ...' He cut her off with a gesture.

'You were only exercising a little typical feminine curiosity ... I know,' he replied. 'But not today. Maybe if you're a good girl, some day I'll tell you all about my rather chequered career—but not today. Today we concentrate on our stomachs and nothing else.'

And then, to her amazement, he thumped his large fist angrily on the table, stirring cutlery and ashtray into a frantic dance of protest.

'Damn it, anyway! I knew I shouldn't have got

shaved and all prettied up; it's too confusing for a young innocent like you.'

Kaarin stared at him. Then, 'That's ridiculous!' she exclaimed. 'And besides, you certainly don't expect me to believe you went through all that just so we could have lunch together without you looking like a ... a ...'

'Hooligan?' He grinned his most engaging smile. 'See? You've just proved your innocence. Most women I know would just automatically assume that such a transformation was entirely in their honour. Which, I might add, it was!'

'Well then, it was totally unnecessary,' Kaarin replied angrily. 'And I hardly take it as a compliment that you'd even remotely consider such a thing necessary in the first place.'

'Why?' There was an evil gleam in his eyes now, a look that held both humour and warning. Kaarin disregarded both.

'Well ... because ... because I liked you just as you were,' she replied.

'And?'

'And ... well, what do you mean, *and*? If I hadn't liked the way you looked I'd have said something before we left,' she said, conveniently ignoring the fact that she'd almost done exactly that.

He grinned mischievously. 'It just doesn't occur to you, I suppose, that I went through *all this* just because I wanted to ... because I preferred to look at least remotely civilised in order to lunch with a lovely lady?'

'Now you're being patronising,' Kaarin snapped. 'Of course it occurred to me. All I'm saying is that—from my point of view—it wasn't necessary.'

A huge hand reached out to capture her own, lifting it across the table to where he could touch his lips to her fingers in a gesture so suddenly intimate that she gasped.

'From my point of view, it was. Now what shall we have for dessert?' he said very softly. End of discussion, and none too soon, because Kaarin suddenly felt terribly vulnerable and confused.

Half an hour later, stuffed to the very brim of her existence with food and wine, she was no less confused. Jack's mercurial mood change—this time back to being suave and charming and . . . fun—did little to allay her confusion, but certainly made it easier to take.

They walked, very slowly indeed, back to the utility, and when Jack insisted on yet a further stroll through the city zoo, Kaarin agreed readily.

They drove back west across the railway line and turned back to the high river bank where the Alexandra Park zoo offered spacious lawns and gardens, huge shade trees and a small variety of wildlife.

In truth it wasn't much of a zoo, especially when compared to the phenomenal Great Western Plains Zoo at Dubbo, which had been one of Kaarin's favourite haunts on warm summer afternoons, but on this day it had Jack Collier beside her, holding her hand as they strolled in silence beneath the massive trees, watching the wallabies and the deer in their enclosure. It was . . . sufficient.

They strolled hand-in-hand in silent communion for perhaps half an hour before Jack finally broke the silence. 'Now,' he said, 'it's time for that shopping trip. I hope you remembered to bring the list, although I doubt we'll be able to get everything that's on it.'

'If we do, you'd best buy another freezer to hold it all,' Kaarin replied. 'We can clean all the beer out of the fridge—or at least most of it—but I certainly can't see wasting perfectly good st . . .'

'Don't say that word!' he cautioned, one finger raised in a gesture of mock severity. 'There's some room in the freezer, and we'll make room for what we buy today even if it means old dog gets to eat like a queen for the next week. My word on it.'

'Yes, sir . . . anything you say, sir!'

And they both laughed as they wandered back to the utility for the drive to the supermarket.

CHAPTER FIVE

KAARIN came awake slowly, wallowing up from her slumber like an exhausted swimmer. Her neck was stiff and one arm was numb, but her first conscious impression was the faint, heathery aroma of after-shave.

After-shave! She flung her head erect, eyes wide open in surprise. Ahead of her, the sun-baked grasslands swept past in a blur until she managed to focus her eyes.

'What's the matter? Having nightmares?' She looked to her right, eyes still wide in her disorientation, to find Jack grinning at her, his teeth brilliant against the darkness of his tan.

'You sure do sleep funny,' he chuckled, returning his eyes to the road ahead. 'Do you always snuggle up to whoever's handy? I sort of feel like an oversized teddy bear.'

Kaarin opened her mouth, then closed it again. What could she reply to *that*? It was all too obvious she'd been napping as he drove, and indeed she'd been sleeping with her head against his shoulder.

'You might have pushed me away,' she finally replied, a little too testily because of her embarrassment.

He shrugged. 'Wasn't bothering me any. You didn't snore loud enough to be a problem.'

'I don't snore.' She tried to sound totally positive, but his only response was an even wider grin.

'That's your story and you stick to it,' he replied. 'But if I was going to live with you, I'd want separate bedrooms—for sleeping, anyway. I like my peace and quiet when I'm trying to sleep.'

'Well then, isn't it handy my camper is so far from

your cabin!' Kaarin snapped, as much angry with herself as with him.

Her venom was wasted. 'Do you always wake up this grouchy?' he asked in response. 'And here I was starting to think you didn't have any faults worth worrying about.'

It was obvious now he was deliberately teasing, but Kaarin's tongue ran away with her despite her knowledge that she was merely falling in with his plans.

'Perfection,' she replied haughtily, 'is boring. But I'm sure you'll be able to put up with my idiosyncrasies for as long as I'll be staying.'

'Just so long as you don't take your bad temper out on the kitchen,' he grinned. 'Now that we've got all the fixings I'm looking forward to seeing if you really cook as well as I reckon. The way to a man's heart is through . . .'

'Oh, spare me the platitudes,' she cut in. 'If you *must* try to ruin what's been an otherwise lovely day, you might at least be original.'

'Oh, all right. I'll stop picking on you,' he grinned. 'Provided you tell me who Doug is.'

Kaarin gasped. Doug! How could he possibly know about . . .

'Your snoring isn't too bad, but you do talk in your sleep,' he replied to her unspoken question. 'He must be somebody special, considering the way you were going on while you were cuddled up to *my* shoulder.' His voice was a leer, though it didn't quite show on his profile as Kaarin looked at him in anguished horror.

'He's . . . it's . . . it is, as you so clearly told me earlier today on a comparable subject,' she replied slowly, mind swirling as she struggled for calmness, 'none of your business.'

'Oh, but I disagree. *You* brought up the subject of Neridah Gregg, thus giving me the option to discuss it or not, since it's entirely my affair. But since you brought up the subject of Doug, whatever his name is, I'm not intruding into something private when I ask for more information. Perfectly acceptable legal procedure, my dear. The witness may be cross-examined on any subject voluntarily brought up by the witness in the first place.'

'Well, you know where you can put that theory, don't you?' Kaarin replied angrily. 'And sideways, while you're at it.'

'Wouldn't fit,' he replied cheerfully. 'But it doesn't matter. He's obviously a past consideration anyway.'

'And just what is that supposed to mean?'

He shrugged. 'Pretty obvious, I should think. If he was a current boy-friend you wouldn't be here.'

'And why not?' She already knew the answer, but she couldn't resist prolonging the argument. Only he fooled her.

'Why not indeed?' he shrugged. 'It wouldn't upset me, but most men aren't nearly so trusting.'

Kaarin was staggered. Having expected a typically chauvinistic reply, she'd already begun marshalling her arguments against it, but they were useless now.

As Jack negotiated the final bit of dirt track to the cabin, she glanced across at him, expecting to see the smirk that would reveal he was having her on, but his face gave no sign of anything but serious consideration to his argument.

'You're not a jealous person, then?' she said finally.

'Nope.' He ran the utility up close to the sagging porch and turned off the engine, then swivelled round to face her. 'When you're older, dear Kaarin, you'll perhaps be lucky enough to realise that jealousy is the curse of a good relationship between any couple. If you're going to really get it together properly, you must build on trust, not a bunch of childishness.'

'I don't have to be older to understand that,' she

retorted. 'For your information, I'm well aware of it already.'

'Ah, then why did you bring up my relationship with Neridah Gregg?'

'Well, certainly not because of . . . of jealousy! That's . . . well, it's just ridiculous.'

'Is it?' His eyes bored into her, reaching clear down to the very centre of her being as if in search of the lie.

'Yes, it is,' Kaarin replied bravely. 'Not only quite ridiculous but insulting as well. Just because you . . . we . . . I think you got quite the wrong idea last night.'

His grin was devilish. 'Do you? I thought it was an excellent idea myself. Well worth repeating, in fact.'

And before she could move he'd reached out to pull her towards him, lifting her chin with his free hand as his mouth descended upon her own. The kiss wasn't harsh or brutal, merely very, very deliberate. And very thorough.

Kaarin's lips melted beneath the pressure, but she kept her arms rigidly by her side, forcing herself not to respond. It was difficult; as Jack crushed her against him, his lips roaming from her mouth to her cheek, caressing the long tresses of her flowing hair, then returning to brush lightly across her eyes, every fibre of her body cried out in response.

'And what do you reckon your Doug would think of that?' he asked after finally releasing her only enough that their faces were mere inches apart.

'Probably about as much as I did,' she sneered, trying to control her trembling. The warmth of the arm around her shoulders, the flexing of his muscles, all threatened to reveal just how affected she really was by his kiss.

'Well, that proves he's out of the picture,' Jack said, then leaned down to kiss her lightly on the tip of the nose. 'Either that or you're the most fickle female I've ever come across.'

And as suddenly as he'd kissed her, he released her, reaching down to tug at the door handle of the utility. 'How's about you getting the coffee on while I unload all this tucker?' he suggested. 'We can continue our discussion over coffee.' And before Kaarin could reply he was out of the truck and leaning into the rear section to pick up one box of groceries.

'You're insufferable!' she muttered, leaping from her own side of the vehicle and stomping up to fling open the cabin door. Inside, she slammed about the kitchen, getting the stove going and preparing the enormous enamel coffee pot.

Jack ignored her temper as he moved back and forth between vehicle and cabin with the groceries, then helped her put things away.

As she'd feared, they had to unload several packets of steak from the freezer to make room for the other things purchased that day, but Jack showed no concern.

'Dog'll be pleased,' he muttered, shifting the steak into the fridge after unloading all but three cans of beer into a carton beside the machine.

Kaarin said nothing, hardly trusting herself to speak. His smug superiority and self-assurance was absolutely maddening, the more so because she couldn't combat it to any real effect.

He had only to touch her and her bones turned to water, and worse, he damned well knew it. It was infuriating!

With the groceries put away, Kaarin poured out coffee for both of them, but she seated herself at the table where she could stare out the window, not wanting to resume her argument in the certain knowledge that she'd only lose.

'Well . . .' Jack's voice broke the silence with the authority of a command.

'Well what?' She didn't bother to turn and look at

him. Surely he could see that she didn't want to discuss the matter any more.

'Well, what's the story on this Doug chap? You're going to tell me sooner or later; it might as well be now.'

'I see no purpose in discussing him at all,' she said coldly. 'So if you don't mind . . .'

'Ah, but I do mind. Did you love him?' It was obvious Jack wasn't going to let it go. Kaarin thought briefly of refusing to answer, then shrugged.

'I thought I did . . . once.'

'What does he do?'

'He's a . . . a writer,' she replied cautiously. And then she did look at Jack, forced into it because of the bray of laughter which issued forth.

'You should never get involved with writers; they're terrible bastards,' he chuckled. 'I'd have thought you'd know better, considering your job.'

'Let's just say it's not a mistake I'm likely to repeat,' Kaarin replied. 'So in future, Mr Collier, I'd be much happier if you'd keep your kisses—and your hands—to yourself.'

'You wouldn't, actually, but I'm not in the mood to argue that right now,' he replied with a knowing grin. 'There are better times for that little discussion. So finish telling me about Doug. Doug who?'

'I really don't want to discuss it,' Kaarin said. 'Why don't you run off and play with your building project or something instead?'

'Tomorrow's soon enough,' he replied with another infuriating grin. 'What did this lad do, dump you as soon as he'd wormed his way into Cleaver's good graces?'

She laughed. 'No, nothing like that. If he had any reason for dumping me, as you so uncharitably put it, I imagine it was solely boredom. I don't think he reckoned a country girl like me was sophisticated enough for him. And he was right, I suppose.'

Jack muttered something Kaarin didn't quite catch, then leapt back to the attack. 'Don't start feeling sorry for yourself,' he jibed. 'He couldn't have had his head very together if he'd reckon you to be boring; I haven't had a dull moment since you arrived.'

'I suppose you expect me to take that as a compliment.'

He shrugged. 'Suit yourself. It certainly wasn't meant to be insulting, anyway.'

'It isn't easy to tell, with your style of compliments,' Kaarin replied archly, 'although I guess I have to agree that it hasn't been exactly boring. Except for the food.'

'Touché! But then we've fixed that, haven't we? So now you'll be able to concentrate on your typing without a single thing to complain about.'

'What you mean,' she countered, 'is that I'll be able to concentrate on my typing whenever I'm not busy cooking, cleaning, feeding the livestock or, from appearances, playing midwife to the dog. You do realise she's almost ready to whelp? I should think tomorrow or the next day.'

'Of course I realise it. Did whatshisname get tired of you before or after he got you into his bed?'

'I don't think that's any of your damned business,' Kaarin replied angrily, shoving back her chair and rising to her feet. 'I also think it's just about time we ended this conversation.'

The tears started even before she reached the door, and as she fumbled blindly for the knob the words escaped unbidden. 'It was . . . such a perfect day. Why did you have to go and spoil it?' she cried as she flung open the door and fled to the questionable sanctuary of her camper. There she was able to cry without the embarrassment of having Jack Collier watch her, but strangely enough her tears didn't last. Anger at his rude questioning quickly swelled up to furnace heat inside her, and for a moment she even considered returning to the cabin and telling him so.

But why bother? It would only give him yet another chance to humiliate her. Or, worse, to continue his interrogation. And it wasn't as if he really cared. He was just trying to satisfy his chauvinistic curiosity.

'Swine!' she screamed aloud, knowing he couldn't hear her but somehow feeling better for shouting it. 'Well to hell with you!' she shouted. 'And you can cook your own damned dinner as well!'

Grabbing up the first book that came to hand—fortunately not one of *his*—she flung herself on to the bunk and tried to lose herself in the story, only to find within minutes that it was poorly written and infantile. Also, the camper was unbearably hot despite the shade of the surrounding trees. Soon she was dripping with perspiration and genuinely uncomfortable.

The next decision was easy. Out of her clothes and into her bikini, then a quick dash across the clearing and down past the building site to the large pool where she'd seen Jack swimming. She flashed up on to the large rock from which he'd dived, and an instant later was tumbling through the startlingly cool water, revelling in its touch on her skin.

It was late enough in the day for her to swim without worrying about sunburn, and she made the most of it, first by swimming hard back and forth across the pool until all of her muscles ached, and then by floating serenely in the centre, hair fanning out around her head and the light breeze cooling her skin.

It was idyllic; the cleansing water gradually sloughed away her bad temper, though it was less successful in easing the unusual feeling of wariness that Jack's questioning had created.

She floated, idly kicking to maintain her position in the slight current of the pool, and pondered her future position in this exceptional relationship. Common logic told her to get a good night's sleep and then use her van to escape back to the relative reality of the outside world. She could easily enough take the tapes with her and do the typing somewhere else—anywhere else—without the disturbance of Jack's interest in her emotional life. He wouldn't like it, of course, but that would be just too damned bad for him!

The only other alternative, and one she knew would please her uncle a great deal more, was to tough it out, stay and get the book typed as quickly and neatly as possible, meanwhile avoiding any further confrontation with Jack and his curiosity. That, she sensed, might not be easy, but it was possible.

The cooling evening breeze made her decide to stave off an immediate decision, and she slowly swam to the edge, towelled herself briskly, and moved back up the slope to her waiting camper van and its illusion of privacy.

She'd just finished changing and had turned on the little gas burner to brew up some tea when a thunderous knock on the door destroyed whatever peace the swim had created.

'Dinner's ready whenever you are,' came the all-too-familiar voice.

'I'm not hungry,' she replied quickly, a lie that sounded false even in her own ears. The exercise of her swim had made her ravenous, though she didn't realise it until the very instant he spoke of dinner.

Jack flung open the door of the van and Kaarin was faced with two angry brown eyes, eyes that seemed to drill straight through her façade.

But it was she who spoke first—or rather, shouted. 'Do you *mind*?' The rest was best unspoken, but she had no doubt Jack had got the message.

'Not in the slightest,' he replied calmly. 'But I *will* mind if you don't stop playing silly games and get yourself over there for dinner. Now!'

'I said I'm not hungry,' she replied hotly. 'Or don't you understand plain English?'

'You want to walk or be carried?' The expression on his face made the ultimatum clear; he wasn't going to leave her any real choice. Kaarin tried for a moment to outstare him, then abruptly abandoned the effort.

'I'll walk, thank you.' And once he'd stepped aside to let her exit the camper, she stalked haughtily along ahead of him, eyes straight ahead but her mind all too conscious that he was striding more slowly behind her and watching with some appreciation the movements of her body beneath the light sundress she'd donned.

She was nearly at the porch, aware that her figure was clearly outlined by the light and the flimsy material of the dress, when awareness struck at her like a hammer blow. She was *naked* beneath the light dress, and from Jack's position that nakedness would be starkly evident. Selfconsciousness altered her stride; she tried to hurry so as to get inside the cabin and away from that revealing silhouette position, and her haste made her stumble at the entrance to the verandah.

Fingers like steel clamped around her arm, steadying her, but before she could wrench herself free he had already removed his hand and was a respectable distance away, not even looking at her.

'Thank you,' she said, the words grating past her lips.

'You're welcome,' he replied with a polite nod, then stepped aside and gestured to her to enter the cabin, and she did.

The meal he had prepared was attractively arranged on the table—a simple salad, the remains of last night's chickens, some olives and pickles. And a bottle of wine and two sparklingly clean glasses.

Very nice, Kaarin thought, but said nothing as Jack held out her chair for her, then seated himself halfway round the table.

Surprisingly, the meal was conducted in silence. Jack made no attempt at conversation, except to ask for the salt and pepper and to check before refilling her wine glass. But it wasn't really a comfortable silence.

Jack shook his head instead of speaking to her when she rose with the intention of making coffee at the end of the meal, then slid from his chair and did the deed himself. It left Kaarin with nothing to do, which rankled because she had begun to feel that she ought to be at least *saying* something. It was ridiculous to be sitting there in baleful silence when she wasn't even really angry any more.

Hurt—yes. She was unable to completely reconcile his intimate questions. But no longer truly angry. If anything, she was more confused by his stoic silence and cold politeness.

But when the coffee was ready, Jack made no attempt to break the silence, and Kaarin simply couldn't. Her mouth was cotton-bud dry, and she found it increasingly difficult even to look at him, much less speak.

When he did speak, it was so unexpected it startled her.

'Well, it's been a long day. I reckon we could both do with an early night, so why don't you trot off to bed? I'll wash up.'

'But you cooked dinner.' The words were out before she thought, and she noticed a glimmer of . . . something . . . in his dark eyes. He was slow replying.

'Hardly what I'd call cooking,' he growled then. 'And tonight I feel like doing dishes, so off you go.' He was already clearing the table, having taken it for granted that Kaarin would obey without question.

Kaarin's first instinct was to argue, disregarding the perverseness of such a move. But her second was simply accept his edict and retire to the camper, because his suggestion of an early night had almost hypnotically made her eyelids heavy and she knew she was more tired than she thought.

'Well ... if you're sure ...' she stammered, only to halt at his brusque nod of acceptance. She was almost at the door, still somewhat unsure of herself, when his voice halted her.

'You'd better take the flashlight to light your way,' he said very quietly. She noticed he didn't turn to face her, but spoke over his shoulder.

'All right,' she replied almost timorously. 'And ... thank you for dinner. And ...' she choked the words out ... 'for lunch, as well. It was quite delicious.'

So nearly an apology, and yet so far from a proper one. Jack merely flashed her an enigmatic grin.

'Any time.' And he'd turned back to his dish-washing. She hardly heard his reply to her whispered, 'Goodnight.'

The blue heeler clambered upright from her position on the porch and accompanied her back to the camper, only turning back as Kaarin reached the vehicle.

'Goodnight, dog,' Kaarin whispered, then opened her mouth again in silent astonishment as her eye caught a flash of light from beneath the camper's main doorway.

It couldn't be! But as she knelt and shone the flashlight directly under the van, the beam revealed that indeed the reflected light was coming from her missing keyring.

She picked up the keys and straightened slowly, her mind awhirl at the implications. So Jack hadn't stolen them after all! Or had he? She thought back to her accusation of that day, a day now seemingly so long ago. He'd obviously not had the keys then; the briefness and skin-tight fitting of his shorts had revealed that all too adequately. But he'd known—suspected?—something. He'd been much too confident, to sure of himself in his replies.

Tonight! Tonight when he'd come to call her to dinner? Had he conveniently deposited the keys there then, giving himself a handy get-out for whenever she found them? It was damningly easy to believe, yet potentially so equally unfair that Kaarin had to examine the situation from every possible angle.

Surely she'd have seen the keys at some earlier time; they'd hardly been greatly concealed beneath the van. Or would she? It was too easy to speculate, too easy to suspect Jack, and yet somehow she *knew* that if he hadn't taken her keys deliberately he'd known where they were.

But what to do now? She was tempted for an instant to return to the house, confront him with the evidence, and try and read his guilt or innocence from his reactions. But could she? She couldn't be sure.

Even as she dithered, her eye caught the movement as the light inside the cabin died. Jack had obviously retired, and whatever opportunity she'd had was gone with the light. She was definitely not going to go hammering on the door now.

The circumstance of the keys bothered her as she herself undressed in the dark and stretched out on the camper's bunk. It was hot, but not unbearable, and though she knew the interior of the cabin would be ten degrees cooler, she never seriously considered wishing she were sleeping there. Such proximity to the sheer physical allure of Jack Collier could be nothing but folly.

By morning, there was no such folly to be considered. Kaarin wakened to the whistle as Jack called up the dog and disappeared over the rise to his building site at dawn, and she slipped over to the cabin, showered and changed without interruption, and immediately began where she'd left off with the typing. She had half a dozen pages done before she thought of coffee and approached the stove to find the coffee already made and a note saying Jack would pass on breakfast.

She sniffed. Obviously he expected her to prepare lunch. Or did he? By eleven-thirty she still hadn't worked that out, but it had disrupted her concentration sufficiently that she thrust herself angrily away from the work and devoted herself to creating a light but substantial meal that would do the two of them.

And when he didn't show by twelve-thirty, she walked to the brow of the ridge and called him.

Her selfconsciousness wasn't shared by the sweat-soaked figure who grinned up at her call, then mimed a reply by pointing first at himself, then at the beckoning coolness of the river below.

'Five minutes?' he called back. 'I'm filthy.'

Kaarin waved her assent, suddenly glad she didn't have to face him directly just yet, and returned to finish her preparations.

And when Jack stepped into the cabin a few minutes later, dripping from his immersion in the river, he gave no sign of being at all embarrassed by Kaarin's selfconsciousness.

'Looks great,' he said, sliding into his place at the table with total disregard for the fact his shorts were soaking wet and his T-shirt no better. He attacked the meal with single-minded efficiency, leaving no real opportunity for conversation.

It wasn't until coffee time, when he left the table for his pipe and tobacco, that Kaarin finally blurted out what she had to say.

'I found my keys last night,' she began, 'under the camper.'

'Umm?' He shrugged a nomcommittal reply. Noncommittal, but conspicuous for the apparent lack of curiosity within it. And his eyes said something—but what?

'I . . . er . . . I'm sorry I got so huffy about it earlier,' Kaarin finally said, mentally cursing her fumbling tongue.

Jack merely shrugged. 'Doesn't matter . . . now,' he replied, then rose abruptly.

'But . . .' It was wasted; he was already gone, walking down off the verandah without a backward glance.

'Damn!' Kaarin allowed her anger to spill out as she vigorously cleaned up the dishes and tidied up the cabin, but it helped in the long run. She was able to return to her typing without the earlier distraction, and by time to start dinner she'd done a most credible amount of work.

She was also hot, sticky, and desperately in need of another swim, but she was hesitant about approaching the pool. What if he were already there? She knew without question that it wouldn't bother Jack Collier one little bit if she found him swimming nude in the pool. But it would bother her, in ways she didn't care to contemplate. Even as she thought of it, her mind conjured up that earlier vision of his virile masculinity poised on the rock, a Greek god body naked in the sunshine.

But oh, how nice it would be to relax in the cooling waters of the river . . .

'I'm for a swim; you coming?' The voice from the doorway startled her, but she hid it well as she turned to find him already on his way to liberate a chilled can of beer from the fridge.

'Yes,' she said without hesitation. 'I'll need only a minute to change.' And as she trotted towards the camper, she thought with some relief that he couldn't possibly expect to swim nude himself after specifically inviting her. At least, she hoped not.

It was a needless fear. Jack waited on the porch, sipping thirstily at the cold brew, until Kaarin stepped from the camper in her bikini with a towel thrown around her shoulders. He finished the drink as she emerged and strode over to join her; obviously he intended to swim in his shorts as he'd done at noon.

'We'll have to remember that dinner will be done at five—or at least I'd best check on it then,' she said as he reached her side, the blue heeler bounding happily at his heels. The bitch was obviously in the final stages of her pregnancy, and to Kaarin's experienced eye she appeared ready to whelp virtually at any moment.

She said as much to Jack, who paused long enough to stroke the dog's head.

'You just remember to do the fateful deed in the whelping box I built you, and not on my lounge chair,' he muttered at the dog, who nuzzled his palm in a gesture that might have signified acceptance of the edict, but as well might not. Kaarin had already noticed the dog's penchant for sleeping on the porch lounge when Jack wasn't using it, and she thought it likely the bitch might choose that familiar resting spot to have her puppies.

Jack didn't speak to her again until they'd both dived into the pool and subsequently found themselves floating side by side in the deep, cold water.

'You sure got a lot of work done today,' he said then, rolling slightly on his side to face her. 'I appreciate it, but there's really no need to drive yourself into the ground. One day more or less isn't going to make a great deal of difference.'

'The sooner it's done the sooner Unc . . . Mr Cleaver will have it on his desk and the happier he'll be,' she replied lightly. 'You will recall that it was supposed to be done the day you telephoned, and the slower I go the later it will be.'

'Okay,' he said. And promptly ducked under water to slide like a great otter beneath the surface as he moved about the pool. Conversation ended—obviously.

Jack left the pool before Kaarin, and as she floated she could see his standing figure up at the building site, leaning lazily on the long handle of a shovel. But by the time she left the water, he was gone, and she felt strangely lonely during the climb back up to her camper.

There was a measure of satisfaction in returning to the cabin to find that her small roast of lamb was turning out exactly right, but Jack was nowhere to be seen as she pulled out the roast for a final basting.

She cleared away the typewriter and papers from the table and was setting their places when he stepped silently in through the door, one finger raised in a gesture for silence. Then, as Kaarin cocked her head in wonder, he repeated the gesture and motioned her to follow him.

He padded noiselessly in bare feet across the rough bare boards of the verandah, and Kaarin felt her suspicions grow as they reached the screened portion he used as a sleep-out. Then she peered past his shoulder and gasped her astonishment.

The blue heeler was comfortably ensconced on the bed, her dark eyes alert to their presence as she looked up and whined softly. Then, oblivious to them, she leaned down and continued to lick the tiny bundle that was already writhing its way towards her udder.

Kaarin felt the heat of Jack's breath as he leaned over to whisper quietly into her ear, 'Can dinner wait? I reckon the next one should be along any minute.'

She nodded a silent acquiescence and they stood quiet, both unwilling to startle the new mother in her labours. Kaarin was so intent on watching the dog that it was some moments before she realised Jack had his arm curled comfortably around her waist, and in the serenity of the scene she never thought to question it. Instead she leaned slightly against him, the better to view the impending birth.

With the first pup safely born, it seemed unlikely their help would be required, and when the second one eased into being a few minutes later, it became evident the blue bitch was coping admirably on her own.

'Let's go eat and leave her alone a bit,' that voice whispered in her ear. 'We'll check again after we've eaten.'

Still cuddled in the crook of his arm, Kaarin backed away from the doorway beside him, both of them moving on tiptoe until they reached the cabin door itself.

'Well . . . so much for my whelping box,' Jack said with a broad grin that belied his surly tone. 'Damned dog! I knew she'd do something like that, but I thought she'd use the lounge.'

His eyes were shining, and Kaarin knew that she, too, must be exhibiting signs of the excitement that raged inside her. Excitement—and a kind of warm, peaceful bliss now that everything seemed to be going right with the birth.

The roast was done to perfection, as were the vegetables, but neither Kaarin nor Jack were in a fit state to properly enjoy the meal. For Kaarin's part, she hardly tasted the food as it went down, and from Jack's constant alertness and periodic glances towards the doorway, she knew he wasn't paying much attention to his meal either.

And they were both silent, though now it was a silence filled with emotion and with a comfortable togetherness, a sharing that transcended whatever differences might have come between them earlier. Watching Jack, Kaarin found herself wanting to go to him, to soothe his worried look and his concern for the dog who had so blithely appropriated his bed for a whelping chamber.

'Come on,' she said finally. 'We can have dessert

and coffee later, if you like. We wouldn't enjoy it right now and I keep thinking I'm missing something.'

The broad grin he threw her was so totally boyish, and so filled with delight at her understanding of the situation, that it was all Kaarin cooould do to keep from crossing the room and hugging him.

He took her hand, cushioning it within his own strong grasp, as they cautiously approached the sleep-out for the second time, pausing at the doorway to let the bitch become accustomed to their presence.

This time when the dog looked up there were four tiny bodies writhing in their search for warmth and food, and already the first two were fully dried and starting to reveal the fluffiness of their short fur.

'I think she's finished,' Kaarin whispered. And sure enough, a moment later the final afterbirth was expelled, disposed of by the mother dog, and the bitch lay back for an instant as the panting and shivering of her labour ceased.

When she leaned forward again to resume cleaning herself and the pups, Kaarin whispered to Jack, 'I think you might go to her, if you want.'

And as if she'd heard and understood, the new mother looked up at Jack and whined her most affectionate greeting, long tongue lolling as she leaned down then to resume her cleansing of the puppies.

Moving slowly so as not to alarm her, Jack stepped over and caressed the bitch, then examined each pup in turn before returning them to the nest. When Kaarin, too, moved closer, a wisp of tongue acknowledged her acceptance.

'One male and three females,' she whispered after her own inspection. 'And they're all perfect ... every one.'

'Which is more than you can say for my bed,' he replied softly. 'But I reckon they might as well stay there until tomorrow. I suppose I should think of it as some kind of compliment, but it's difficult just now.'

'Oh, pooh! You're just as pleased as if you'd made them yourself,' Kaarin replied saucily.

'Umm,' he replied as they returned to the kitchen. 'I just wish we'd had kids here to have watched it. Great thing for kids. I doubt if I'll ever forget the first litter I saw born.'

'Me either,' Kaarin replied, but it was an automatic reply. Most of her mind was still trying to fathom his remark about wishing 'we had kids here'. Surely it was just a way of expressing himself, she thought. What made it so poignant was that she'd been thinking exactly the same thing, only in her case she feared there was more to it than just an expression.

She might spend half her time being angry with Jack Collier, but the other times seemed to more than make up for it. And to think of having his children—that was the kind of thinking best avoided from the start.

Not an easy task when Jack insisted upon opening two bottles of wine to toast the happy event. 'You can even get tipsy if you like,' he chided. 'I won't take advantage, promise. Unless of course I'm provoked.'

'And I think we spend too much time provoking each other, though not quite in the way you mean,' Kaarin replied with a grin. 'A truce—at least for tonight—would be more than welcome.'

'So a truce it is,' he responded, filling their glasses and then lifting his own in salute. 'And here's to motherhood!'

'To motherhood,' Kaarin agreed, wishing he hadn't looked at her in quite *that* fashion when proposing the toast. His dark eyes had an ability to see right inside her, it seemed, and truce or not she didn't feel totally comfortable with her own feelings about this undeniably attractive man.

They drank their first glasses of wine in a sort of companionable silence. Kaarin presumed Jack was thinking about the puppies, but her own mind was less fixed. It kept returning again and again to his remark, and to the unfathomable gleam in his eye when he'd proposed his toast.

He made no move to get physically closer to her, seeming content to sit across the table where he could watch her, talk to her. And when he did begin to speak it was of innocuous things—the puppies, pets he'd had as a child, some of the work he'd done as a journalist before shifting over from factual journalism to pure fiction.

'Some people can't reconcile such a change,' he said with what could only be called a wicked grin.

Kaarin grinned before replying. 'I thought all you journalists were little more than frustrated authors,' she retorted. 'Besides, there's a very fine dividing line between fact and fiction these days.'

'Well, that's true enough—although most journalists who become authors tend to shift into comparable work, writing non-fiction because that's what they've been trained for. Or, at best, fiction that's really only thinly-disguised fact. I switched for different reasons.'

'Such as?' Kaarin wasn't being patronising; she was truly interested, but Jack threw her a cautious glance and seemed to think rather carefully before replying.

'Escape,' he said then, and closed his mouth around the world. 'I'm a drop-out—or at least that's what they'd call me if I wasn't making so damned much money.'

Kaarin stifled a giggle. Drop-out! There could hardly be a more fitting description for the Jackson Collier she'd met in the beginning—months overdue for a haircut, unshaven, and wearing clothes that were closer to drop-off than drop-out. That thought made her giggle even louder, and at his baleful scowl she hurriedly explained the reason for her laughter.

'But I'm not laughing *at* you,' she assured him. 'It's

just that—well, I can't quite see you as the drop-out you think of yourself as. Fiction, to be successful, has to be closely related to fact, or at least to the possible. I think you've just shifted the emphasis of your life.'

'And I think you should have been a diplomat,' he replied, the scowl less evident but not entirely dissipated.

He paused, and then, 'I remember now you saying something snooty about Neridah Gregg and me when we were in that restaurant. Maybe you'd like to tell me now just what spurred that on—because I know damned well it wasn't curiosity. More likely there've been interesting rumours that I've gone bush to nurse a broken heart, or some such rubbish.'

Kaarin couldn't lie about it. Indeed, the expression on her face revealed the truth of his accusation without her saying a word.

'Hah! I thought as much,' he snarled. 'And I suppose my old mate Bill Cleaver has been helping the rumours along?'

'He has not! In fact he told me himself they were a load of rubbish,' Kaarin replied. 'He said ... he said she wasn't woman enough to send you off to any ... hermitage, if you must know.'

'Did he? Then I apologise for maligning the old duck,' Jack laughed. 'Nice to see some people have faith in me. And what do you think, dear Kaarin?'

'I ... don't know anything about it,' she replied hastily. And not very convincingly, 'Nor do I especially want to. It isn't any of my business.'

This time his laugh was genuine, and there wasn't a hint of bitterness that Kaarin could detect. Instead he leaned back in his chair and regarded her with an owl-like stare.

'I'd have thought you'd be ... curious ... at least, especially since you've been exiled to this particular wilderness to share it with me,' he said provocatively.

'Are you sure old Bill didn't send you out here to mend my tattered heart, get me straightened out and back on the track to a more contemporary life-style? More books, more money, more publicity to help sell the books? And don't look so innocent, dear Kaarin. You're a very attractive woman and you know it—and I wouldn't put such a scheme past old Bill Cleaver, even without him bothering to clue you into what he was scheming about.'

'I don't know anything about his schemes, but I can assure you there's no such scheme in *my* mind,' Kaarin replied cautiously. 'I'm here to help you finish your book and get it typed, and then I'm off to the Gold Coast for a well-deserved holiday. Nothing more.'

Jack looked at her, eyes hard with undisguised speculation. 'So anything romantic that might develop between us would be purely accidental, eh? You know, I almost believe you.'

Kaarin spat out the bait. Her voice in reply was silky smooth and non-aggressive. 'I certainly hope so,' she said. 'And when I've left—with nothing having developed—you'll have your proof.'

'Proof!' Jack laughed and shook his head meaningfully. 'All *that* would prove is that I really have gone bush, or worse, right round the twist. Come on, Kaarin, you may be a trifle naïve, but you're not stupid. Do you really expect us to continue under these circumstances of rather enforced proximity and have me just ... ignore you? I know I'm getting on, but I'm not that old.'

Kaarin met his stare across the table and shivered inwardly. Despite the distance between them and the solid physical presence of the table as a barrier, his eyes caressed her face like the gentlest of fingers, and she could almost feel his touch upon her.

'I would remind you that you managed to ignore me rather well during the first few days I was here,' she said coldly. 'I see no reason for it not to continue.'

'You are naïve,' he growled, 'if you think what I was doing was ignoring you while I was giving you generous applications of sunburn cream...' his eyes dropped to the cleft of her bosom, the stirring hollow of her throat, '... and undressing you ... and tucking you into bed...'

'Stop it!' Kaarin's voice was a squeal of protest not at what he was saying, but at the way he said it. His voice had become a hypnotic, sensual extension of himself, and whenever it touched her she quivered with a desire that frightened her by its strength.

She closed her eyes for a second in her anguish, and Jackson Collier struck like an angry tiger snake. When Kaarin's eyes blinked open again he was before her, his hands reaching out to take her by the shoulders as he lifted her from her chair.

'Stop? Not on your life, young Kaarin. I've only just started.'

His voice stopped as his lips touched hers with the searing kiss of a branding iron, forcing her mouth to open like a softened wound as his arms crushed her against him. This was not lovemaking; it held no tenderness, no compassion. It was an assault on her senses, designed to arouse.

'Only ... started...' his voice hissed in her ear as his lips brushed the lobe in a startlingly intimate caress. Suddenly he held her away from him so as to peer directly into her eyes, locking the contact with one hand on her trembling chin.

'And I won't stop, Kaarin. Not until I know for positive certain that whatever is between us is totally innocent, as you'd have me believe—or something sneaky being engineered by your boss. Meanwhile, I'm just going to enjoy it.'

His lips moved closer again, but Kaarin managed to wedge one elbow against his chest, holding him away long enough to grunt, 'There's nothing . . . sneaky. In fact there's nothing . . . between us at all. Now let me . . .'

'Nothing?' And with sheer physical force he levered her elbow away and once again claimed her lips. His arms were so tight around her that she could hardly breathe, and yet somehow his fingers remained free to stroke the small of her back, the smooth contours of her shoulderblades. And his mouth roamed over hers like an avenging barbarian conqueror, taking and giving at the same time.

The tempo shifted, became softer, more intimate and less harsh as Kaarin's struggles turned against her. The closeness of his body, the pressure against her of taut, masculine muscle, the expert touch of his lips all worked to strip away her defences.

'Nothing?' This time it was a whisper, a voice out of time that slid insidiously inside her mind as his lips moved down her cheek to the hollows of her throat, the softness lower down.

Kaarin's fingers, tangled in the coarse hair of his chest, moved by their own volition, shifting, touching, exploring the play of muscles as his body shifted against her. When his lips moved down to brush aside the half-opened blouse she'd slipped into after swimming, her hands slid up to wrap around his neck, her lips touching his hair, her nostrils drinking in the clean, heady scent of him. She was aware of his fingers gently opening the rest of the blouse, sliding inside to cup her breasts, each in their turn, stroking them to a taut readiness.

His lips moved up again to claim hers, eagerly now and without the harshness, the hurt of before. Now his mouth was gentle, demanding and yet giving, welding them together as his fingers toyed with her swollen breasts.

When he lifted her towards the daybed, her mouth

opened to protest, but he closed it with his own, and no other part of her body objected to the new surges of passion as he laid her down and slid down beside her, one arm beneath her head and the other roving trails of ecstasy over her body.

Her own hands were exploring again, flaunting the dying directives from a mind drugged by passion as they moved across his stomach, the still-damp cloth of his shorts to the muscles of his thighs. And part way back as his fingers deftly moved at the waistband of her terry-towelling shorts.

Surrender! Her body was demanding it and her mind lost all ability to resist as the soft towelling slid away under his expert fingers. Her body was powerless to resist, flowing on a sea of passion without rudder or direction as his hands, his lips, his body moved over her.

Surrender! The body screamed it and her mind abandoned her. She let herself sink into the depths of their mingled passions, softening and flowing into something that yearned only to become one with him.

CHAPTER SIX

AND then, as she poised on the brink of rapture, something changed. Infinitesimal at first, but a subtle alteration of Jack's lips, hands, body, and his bond with her combined to draw her away from that brink.

There was no harshness, only a terribly gentle shift in direction. He still kissed her, his hands still moved across her body in waves of infinite pleasure, but he was drawing her back, ever so slowly, to reality.

Their bodies surrendered reluctantly to the gradual, sensuous parting, her breasts lost some of their rigidity as his caresses became increasingly less passionate, though no less gentle, no less caring.

The aching need in her, a need that had been a raging fire of desire, slowly subsided to small coals and then to only a comfortable warmth. And her mouth tasted once again the true taste of his lips, untainted by the demanding needs of a few moments earlier.

'Are you all right now?' It was a whisper, a tender, gentle question as one might query a child with a skinned knee.

Kaarin couldn't speak; but she nodded her assent and then confirmed it with her lips as he kissed her lightly before sliding his body away from her own. Once on his feet he held her, steadying her as she rearranged her clothing.

'Come now and I'll walk you back,' he said, reaching for the flashlight beside the door but still holding her with one hand.

'Wh-why . . .?' She never got the question fully out. Jack shook his head, eyes so alive with a weary, gentle compassion that she couldn't argue.

'Come,' he said, guiding her towards the door. 'And

don't ask silly questions.'

There was no longer a strangeness between them, no longer any sense of conflict. He put his arm around her as they strolled silently towards the camper, and Kaarin snuggled against him in a comfort that was both asexual and totally sexual, yet somehow right.

And when he opened the camper and helped her step inside, then kissed her still-soft mouth, she returned the kiss with genuine warmth and felt the honesty of his kiss.

Once she was in bed, now strangely lonely and yet assured of the rightness of her being there, her mind began trying to unravel what had transpired. Jack had won! He had claimed her, body and soul, brought her to the point of no return with an expertise that was so far beyond her experience she could only marvel at it. And yet he had backed away. He—not Kaarin herself. Without rejection, because he had not rejected her.

It was as if he had led her to the edge of a cliff and even held her hand as she peered over it, then gently guided her back to seek a safer way down.

She thought of his earlier accusations, but only briefly. They no longer mattered now, and she knew it. As surely as she knew that she loved him. Loved him!

But dared she believe it was a love he fully returned? Or was his unwillingness to take advantage simply a gesture—a moral consideration she couldn't quite deal with?

She slipped into a restful, calming sleep, smiling to herself. Tomorrow would tell her. Just what, she wasn't sure, but it would be nothing to hurt her, because she knew now that Jackson Collier would not hurt her.

And she woke with the same unshakeable certainty, peering out to see the pale light of dawning with a new clarity, a new sharpness. The whole world seemed to be singing for her; even the raucous hilarity of the kookaburras held a note of laughter shared.

She wanted to run, leaping in the serene happiness that filled her morning. She wanted to shout out her well-being. But at half past four in the morning both ideas seemed mildly extreme. What she could do, however, was go for a swim.

She picked up her towel, dry after a night on the back of a seat in the camper, then picked up her bikini and looked at it speculatively.

And with a joyous laugh she flung the wispy garment down on the seat, grabbed up the towel and ran across the clearing, down the hillside and paused for an instant on the rock. *His* rock. Dropping the towel, she dived neatly into the depths of the pool.

She swam, luxuriant in her new-found freedom and sensually aware of how the lapping waters caressed her body. Not quite like *his* caresses, but enjoyable enough. Swirling her mane of blonde hair around, she dived deep into the pool, rising and blowing like a demented porpoise, then diving again.

Until once she came up for air to see a tall, muscular figure standing like a bronzed statue upon the rock, a figure that regarded her nakedness with one eyebrow raised in surprise before raising a hand in silent salute.

Kaarin grinned and waved in reply, miming her wish that he join her, and then dived deep under the waters and stayed as long as she could. She reached the surface and gulped in fresh air in a great gasp that turned to a squeal as hands closed about her waist and lifted her half out of the water.

She was pirouetted, spun in those strong hands like a doll, and then lowered so that lips like velvet could deposit a friendly, non-passionate good morning kiss upon her own smiling mouth.

'Good morning,' he said, his entire face smiling the welcome.

'And to you,' she replied happily, circling her arms around his neck and letting the current swirl her against him.

The dark eyes flickered slightly as their bodies met and then drifted slightly apart. And Kaarin's happiness was touched by the feel of his shorts against her naked hip.

'I love your new swimsuit,' he said very quietly, and the warmth in his eyes reassured her. 'But don't you think it's just a bit provocative?'

'Not especially,' she replied, her eyes laughing at him. 'Why? Do you think so?'

'Enough that I would appreciate it if you'd go back to wearing the old one,' he replied quite seriously. 'Otherwise I might not be responsible for my reactions.'

'Oh,' Kaarin pouted prettily. This was fun! She leaned closer, eyes only inches from his. 'And what would you do?'

'You really want to know?' There was a cynical gleam in his eye now, a warning she ought to heed—but she didn't.

'Yes,' she whispered. And moved even closer to him. The current had drifted them over against one edge of the pool, and both could stand easily on the pebbly bottom.

'All right,' Jack grinned. 'But don't say I didn't warn you.'

And before she could resist he had lifted her like a child in his arms and strode dripping from the pool to where a huge rock provided a handy seat. Braced upon it, he tumbled her across his knee and laced into her with his free hand.

She squealed at the first blow, squalled angrily at the second, and felt the tears begin at the third . . . the last. Then he tumbled her upright again and kissed her thoroughly.

'Now go get some clothes on and stop playing silly games,' he grinned, eyes gentle as his touch at her waist. 'The price is too high—for both of us.'

When he released her, Kaarin's first instinct was to slap him silly, but one look into those dark eyes quickly forestalled such a move. Her bottom tingled a warning against further provocation.

So she took the only alternative and strode haughtily back to where her towel awaited her, vividly aware that his eyes were following each movement of her body, but that he'd set a limit on the relationship and would stick to it.

'And get some breakfast started,' he shouted as she scurried up the slope towards the cabin. 'There's work to do, you know?'

She turned in her tracks and flipped two fingers at him in a gesture of universal understanding, then had to giggle as he returned it with a broad, totally friendly grin. Her anger evaporated by the time she'd slipped into shorts and a T-shirt, defiantly omitting to bother with a bra.

Then she strolled over to the cabin and had bacon, eggs, fruit juice, toast and coffee almost ready when Jack, still dripping from the pool, sauntered into the kitchen.

'Smells great, just like you,' he grinned, reaching for a towel and rumpling it through his dripping hair. Then he walked over and stood behind her, as she turned away to concentrate on the eggs.

Hands slipped around her waist and lips slid hauntingly across the back of her neck, their touch rousing, yet only mildly so.

'Sorry I had to lick you this morning,' he whispered in her ear, 'but there's only so much temptation I'm game to face, and the time's just not right . . . yet.'

Yet! That single word drove off her demons, kicked out every doubt she'd felt. Kaarin's heart thrilled to his touch, his words, his presence.

'I'm sorry too,' she said over his shoulder. 'I was a tease, I know. I won't do it again.'

His lips touched her neck in brief assent, then he walked back to sit at the table, where she joined him once breakfast was ready.

They ate, shared the washing up, then crept to the sleep-out for a quick check on the pups. The blue bitch readily accepted Jack's invitation for a relieving walk, and while they were outside Kaarin transferred the pups to the whelping box and stripped away the soiled linen from the bed.

The dog returned, gave Kaarin a rather snooty look at the interference, then settled happily enough in the box and began to feed the tiny wriggling puppies.

A few minutes later, Jack strode away down the hill to his building site and Kaarin sat facing the typewriter, headphones in place and her fingers ready to begin another day's work. They were together for a brief swim before lunch, and when her fingers became weary and her vision blurred about three o'clock, she put on her great huge hat and strolled down to visit him at his work.

It was a pattern they followed more or less during the week that followed, a pattern of shared work, little shared intimacies, but with the undiscussed climax of it all still hovering in the wings.

Kaarin slept alone; Jack shared the sleep-out with the bitch and her pups. But in all other respects it seemed to Kaarin as if they were married. They kissed good morning, always goodnight, and often at unexpected times Jack would rouse her with a touch that held such tenderness, such perfect emotional balance, that she went all weepy inside.

And on the Wednesday, when he drove quickly into Gayndah to get vitamins for the nursing bitch and check on his mail, she felt lonely and strangely vulnerable during the scant two hours he was away.

He brought her a present—an enormous crate of the succulent oranges for which the Gayndah district was famous and a flask of scented shampoo wrapped in a pretty bow.

'No mail for you,' he announced. 'Are you sure anybody knows you're here?'

'We know. Who else matters?' she replied happily.

He shrugged, and she saw for the first time a hint of something in his eyes that showed he was troubled. 'Some people know I'm here, worse luck,' he growled then. 'And what's worse, I've got to fly to Sydney for a couple of days.'

He looked at the instant dismay in her eyes and stepped over to kiss her affectionately on the tip of the nose.

'It isn't the end of the world,' he said gently. 'Just an obligation I can't ignore. I'll drive to Bundy tomorrow and fly down, and I should be back by Sunday night at the latest.'

Kaarin fought off the black depression that fluttered hungrily around her heart. 'Well, that's no problem,' she replied with forced brightness. 'It'll give me even more time to type and I might even have the book finished by the time you get back—provided I don't get orders from the boss to make bricks instead!'

During the past week she had found intense pleasure in moulding the heavy adobe bricks, mixing and tamping the mud into a special steel form Jack had had built. In fact, her input into the construction of the house had given her nothing but pleasure, because of the sharing and the opportunity to be with him.

'Well, don't work too hard,' he replied absently. 'I'll drop the stuff you've already done to Cleaver, and that'll keep him off our backs for a while.'

'I'll be just as glad to get the typing over with,' Kaarin said at dinner that evening. 'Much as I enjoy reading your books, and this is the best yet, I think I'd rather do my reading after it's printed and bound.'

'Too right!' Jack's grin was infectious. 'But at least now you can understand why I use tapes, which has to be the smartest thing I've ever done. Once I get a book worked out in my head, there's no way I can type fast enough to keep up. Last time I tried it I lost an entire chapter in one place.'

Kaarin stretched and yawned, her entire body feeling languorous. The sheer physical effort of mixing the twenty-kilogram adobe bricks had caused her some stiffness the first few days she'd tried it, but now her afternoon stints served only to guarantee a good night's sleep for a body that fairly glowed with health and fitness.

'Who do you have to see in Sydney?' she asked, more from a point of making idle conversation than because she was particularly curious.

'Cleaver, for one,' Jack replied. 'I'm sure it'll please him no end to find most of the book finished and his number one girl almost ready to return to the fold.'

'Not till I've had my holiday,' Kaarin retorted. 'That is one agreement I intend to make sure he keeps.'

'Two weeks of lazing in the Gold Coast sun while I'm slaving over a hot brick machine, and I'll bet you never even give me a thought,' Jack mused. 'Sure you wouldn't like to stay and make bricks instead?'

The question so mirrored her own thoughts that Kaarin had to avert her eyes lest he see too deeply into her soul. It was equally difficult to maintain a straight face as she answered him lightly.

'That depends on what you're paying. Combination cooks, housekeepers and bricklayers' labourers don't come cheap, you know.'

'You're not wrong,' he muttered, and Kaarin was surprised at the note of ... bitterness, could it be? ... in his voice. Then it disappeared. 'I'll think about it while I'm gone,' he said with unexpected enthusiasm. 'Maybe if I bring you a nice present from the Big Smoke you'll consider bringing your price down to something I can manage.'

Was it a hint? Kaarin didn't know exactly how to interpret the remark, and in her silence Jack broke in to further confuse things.

'Although the way you're going, I'm likely to get back and find you've built the house without me. Well, just you remember, my lady, that I'll have bunyips watching while I'm gone, and if I find out you've been running around without your hat on in the sun, I'll tan your hide for you properly.'

Kaarin laughed at the thought of hordes of bunyips—mythical swamp monsters of Aboriginal legend—peeping from behind every tree. 'Goodness, I'll have to stop swimming in the nude, then,' she giggled. 'I wouldn't want to give your bunyips a complex or anything!'

'I don't know why not; you've already given me a complex by doing it,' Jack retorted with a knowing grin. 'Now come and help with the dishes before my mind gets the better of me. I'd like to be able to make this trip with a clear conscience.'

'For somebody who writes such lurid fiction, you sure are old-fashioned,' said Kaarin. 'I thought it was us girls who are supposed to be all shy and retiring and ... and *thing*. You're a prude, Jackson Collier; that's what you are.'

'And you're a little tease who's just spoiling for a licking,' he snapped. 'So get your hands in the sink, woman, and be glad I'm a patient man.'

But when they sat together on the porch while Jack had his final pipe of the evening, listening to the night sounds and touching without touching in an aura of sublime peace for Kaarin, she found herself wondering how Jack would react to seeing Sydney and all his high-powered acquaintances again. Would he be seeing Neridah Gregg? she mused, and shivered unconsciously.

'What's the matter, somebody walk over your grave?' he asked, and she turned with alarm. Even though physically separated from her, he'd felt the shiver. It was enough to make her shiver again, though she covered it with a saucy reply to his question.

It wasn't until she was alone in her camper bunk, lips still warm from his goodnight kiss, that she thought of Neridah Gregg once more.

They were the kind of thoughts that even Kaarin had to admit were uncharitable and childishly petty, but she couldn't seem to turn her mind off, and the entire night was spent tossing and turning in the grip of a nightmarish jealousy.

Jack was uncharacteristically sombre himself when they sat down to breakfast with the sun only half awake in the eastern sky, but he tried his best to appear cheerful without fooling anyone. Kaarin did better; she managed to fool Jack, if not herself, into believing his trip to Sydney wasn't upsetting her unreasonably.

They chatted about totally inconsequential things, both tacitly avoiding discussion of the trip, or who he'd be seeing, or what he might be doing. It was only when he'd levered himself into the driver's seat of the battered old utility, suitcase on the seat beside him, that the trip was mentioned.

'Don't plan tea for me on Sunday night,' he said almost as an aside. 'I don't know for sure, now I've thought about it, that I'll even get here until quite late. In fact I might even have to be a day or so later, depending on a couple of things—so if that happens, don't panic. You've got enough tucker to last six months and dog food for nearly that long . . .'

'I am not the type of girl who panics,' Kaarin interrupted. 'Now go, or you'll end up missing your plane.

Then we'd see panic.'

'Only at the Sydney end of things,' he replied with a grin that could only be called morose. 'Oh, dammit, Kaarin; I wish I didn't have to go . . .'

And even as he spoke, one arm snaked out to curl about her waist, hauling her to him like a fish on a line. His lips found hers in a kiss so filled with need and wanting that her entire body vibrated in response. It ended far too quickly as the same arm thrust her away and slammed shut the truck door.

'Be good,' he said, and the wheels spun as he accelerated rapidly down the narrow path through the trees.

Be good! Whatever else could he expect? she wondered. Except, perhaps, lonely. And she was that already, despite the knowledge it was an expectable and acceptable problem. Nobody can expect to live their lifetime in someone else's pocket, and Kaarin's rural background made her somewhat more aware of that than many city girls might be.

So she'd be lonely, she thought as she returned to the cabin and her waiting typewriter. But only for a few days, just enough to make the reunion that little bit sweeter. And maybe with the typing done and the freedom to spend her days outside helping Jack with the house, maybe then they'd be able to sort themselves out properly.

For her own part, Kaarin needed little sorting out. She loved Jackson Collier with all the love she had to give, and there was no question in her mind about the truth of that.

The problem, if there was one, was in Jack himself. Kaarin's intuition told her that he was in love with her, or so close to it as made no never mind. But she also realised he was intellectually skirting the commitment, unwilling to actively confront his deepest emotions and yet equally unwilling to treat Kaarin with sufficient casualness to deny his feelings.

But would anything really change upon his return? Or would she be forced to take her Gold Coast holiday after all, since she obviously couldn't stay on here without a fairly direct invitation? For all the vivid promiscuity in his books, Jack was obviously much more conservative in his personal affairs, at least in those that mattered.

'Or do I matter at all?' she mused aloud, then brushed the question aside unanswered and locked her mind in on the work at hand.

Once her mind and fingers had become properly co-ordinated, the typing went exceptionally quickly. She became totally engrossed, and during the next two days she paused only to nibble at cold left-overs in the fridge, drink incessant cups of instant coffee, which saved her having to fire up the ancient wood stove, and to sleep in a series of brief catnaps when eystrain forced rest upon her.

She typed 'The End' at three o'clock on Saturday morning, slept twelve hours straight and woke up with a silly but undeniable craving for steak and eggs.

She chuckled at the irony of it while fumbling in the kindling box for paper and small scraps of wood to get the old range going, but the chuckle was throttled as her eyes inexplicably focused on one of the envelopes just as she was about to thrust it into the fire box.

The heavy, pale-blue parchment paper was sufficient to draw a modicum of attention, but what had caught her eye was the specially-printed return address label in the top left corner.

'Neridah Gregg,' it began, followed by a Sydney address that blurred before Kaarin's astonished eyes. In her mind she could see Jack casually flinging his discarded mail into the kindling box, and although she didn't remember this particular envelope it must have been part of the mail which had forced his rush departure.

It was the letter in this envelope that forced it, a squeaky, jealous voice inside her whispered. And the voice ignored her immediate protestations, conjuring up horrific visions of Jack and the beautiful socialite in situations she couldn't bear to visualise.

She stared at the envelope for what seemed like hours, her fingers and jealous demon telling her the letter was still inside, merely awaiting her decision to read it and confirm or deny her worst fears. Then she set it aside and touched a match to the kindling.

It took all her will power to go through the motions of cooking up her steak and eggs, a meal that turned to sawdust as it passed her lips. The fancy that seemed so romantically ludicrous only minutes before now appeared only ludicrous—and increasingly demeaning.

Half a dozen times during the meal she was forced to stop eating and brush away tears that blurred her vision before trickling tormented pathways down her cheeks. And whenever the tears weren't puddling, the soft blue envelope drew her eyes like a magnet while the monster in her brain cried out at her to open it, read whatever was inside.

It would be so easy, so horribly easy. And so wrong! To invade Jack's privacy—anybody's privacy—so deliberately, so crassly, went against all Kaarin's standards. But the demon inside her, the dirty little green-eyed demon of jealousy, had no morals. And it had an increasingly vulnerable subject on which to work its evil.

Kaarin leaned forward on to the kitchen table, head in hands that trembled with the intensity of the war within her. The pressure of her fingers against her eyes created a kaleidoscope of lights that whirled and flashed in patterns without rhyme nor reason. Her tortured mind seemed to follow the lights, whirling without hope of a decision, dancing to the haunted music of the demon jealousy.

She loved Jack, but dared she trust him? Dared she *not* trust him, for what kind of love could not trust? And yet, the evidence . . .

Enough! She thrust herself unsteadily erect and lurched towards the stove, one hand outstretched with claw-like fingers that clutched at the hideous envelope. She lifted it, stared at the return address with eyes reddened and sore, then quickly threw open the firebox door and flung the envelope into the scorching flames.

Once, as she coldly watched the fire nibble at the edges of the envelope and its unknown contents, her hand reached unconsciously for the tongs with which she could rescue it. But only once, and then the urge wasn't strong enough to make resisting impossible. Then it was too late in any event. The flames consumed the letter even more quickly than tormenting jealousy had vainly eaten at her sense of right and wrong.

As the final edges of the letter and envelope slid into grey-white ash, Kaarin breathed a deep sigh of self-satisfaction. She had won, and the victory, although vaguely hollow, like her heart, still had its share of pleasure.

When Jack returned, she would have at least the personal satisfaction of knowing herself worthy of loving him, and of being loved if that was to be. Had she read the letter, love would have died—slaughtered by emotions she no longer dared to acknowledge within herself.

She spent the remainder of the day at the building site, using harsh physical exercise to try and exorcise the green-eyed demon that still lurked in her mind, and largely she succeeded. It wasn't until long after dark, when she tried to sleep, that the demon revived.

Sunday's dawn found her back at the building site, eyes grainy after an uneasy night but with her mind somewhat eased by second thoughts about the affair.

And she stayed any further thoughts against Jack's relationship with Neridah Gregg by sheer physical labour, hauling pails of water from the river, puddling the mud into the correct consistency and trampling it into the mould brick by brick until much of the available flat ground was covered by heavy bricks drying in the sun.

She worked straight through the hottest part of the day, pausing occasionally to smear herself with sunscreen and always sheltering beneath the huge hat that Jack had bought her. When she ran out of space for new bricks, she created space by laboriously stacking all the ones Jack had moulded earlier, bricks now solid and thoroughly dried by the scorching sun.

But at four o'clock she stopped, and returned to the cabin to feed the dog and the chickens and begin her preparations for Jack's return. A large pork loin roast stuffed with raisins and herbs went into the oven at five o'clock, the crackling carefully scored and spiced and laid on a rack to cook by itself. Potatoes, beans and a mixture of turnip and carrots were ready for their place in the cooking when she took herself to the river and slid naked into the cooling waters for half an hour of sheer relaxation.

By eight o'clock she was completely prepared, her hair dried and brushed until it shone, her large blue eyes enhanced by just a slick of eye-shadow and her lips warmed by the palest of pink lip-glosses.

By careful manipulation of the elderly wood stove, she had arranged it so that the roast would be ready by ten o'clock, or could be speeded up to finish earlier if Jack arrived early. And, she thought, it could be kept warm and succulent until eleven o'clock if need be.

She couldn't unfortunately, control her thoughts as easily as she did the oven. By nine o'clock she was pacing inside the kitchen and an hour later concern and apprehension were fast giving way to frustrated anger. At eleven, she dined alone, chewing the cardboard-flavoured meat and accoutrements and wondering how anything could look so delectable and taste so awful.

And at midnight she had to accept that he simply wasn't coming that night—a fact that neither her hopes nor wishes could alter.

Jealousy and genuine concern fought for control of her mind through the remainder of a sleepless night, a night spent pacing the kitchen and alternately sitting in rigid discomfort on *his* lounge on the porch. Monday morning was no better, and by noon she could stand it no longer.

Gathering up the remaining chapters of manuscript, she drove her camper to Gayndah and put them in the mail with a short note to her uncle.

Unable to marshal her thoughts properly, she wrote only that she was starting her holiday and would see him in a fortnight. She mentioned nothing about where or how she would spend the holiday, because she no longer felt any certainty about it herself.

That all depended on Jack, and who could guess what his attitude would be? Kaarin's own mind was like a maniac pendulum, swinging from jealous anger one instant to black despair and worry the next. Was he sick? Was he snugly ensconced somewhere with Neridah Gregg? Was she being totally unfair, and would she find on his return that the delay—which he'd predicted in advance—was purely business and nothing else?

She briefly debated telephoning her uncle. She had a proper excuse with the mailing of the manuscript, but she knew Bill Cleaver too well. He'd quickly read enough from her voice to guess at least something of the problem, and that was something Kaarin simply couldn't face.

No, she decided, she would simply have to await

Jack's return and let his explanations or lack of them confirm or deny the growing concerns that tortured her mind. Only how much longer would she be forced to wait? Would he come today, or would she be on tenterhooks until tomorrow ... the next day?

The thought of days of waiting was unbearable. She just couldn't do it. There was nothing with which to fill the time; she'd made so many bricks there was no room to mould any more, she'd read everything in both camper and cabin, and there was simply nothing else to do.

'Oh, damn you anyway, Jack Collier,' she muttered, and immediately felt guilty in case he arrived back at the cabin before her with a perfectly logical explanation. She turned in as her eye caught a newsagent sign, and she spent several minutes browsing idly through the various magazines and paperbacks before selecting a number to take along with her.

Nothing heavy; she knew herself well enough to realise her current state of mind wouldn't allow serious concentration. But there was one fashion magazine she fancied, and four light but thick romances which would help to pass the time.

She had just paid for her choices and was waiting for the clerk to wrap them when a man appeared beside her and spoke to the clerk about the weekend papers he'd forgotten to collect the day before. The man was obviously a local and the clerk reached beneath the counter to hand up a thick sheaf of newspapers before returning to Kaarin's parcel.

The man laid them down as he searched his pockets for change, and as Kaarin idly looked down at the headlines, a picture seemed to leap from the page at her.

Her eyes widened as icy fingers clutched at her heart. The picture was too clear for a mistake, and the headline 'Socialite and Author Together Again' confirmed what her eyes couldn't comprehend.

There was Jackson Collier, resplendent in dinner suit and spanking white shirt, his arm around the glamorous Neridah Gregg. Kaarin gulped down her rising bile.

Nerveless fingers took the parcel from the clerk, who looked at her strangely but made no comment. Vacant eyes somehow steered her from the shop and down the street to where the van was parked. Unlocking the vehicle, Kaarin threw her parcel into the passenger seat and stood trembling, arms bracing her against the side of the van as she fought the heaving inside her.

Something inside was screaming, pulsating, trying to fight free. She choked down her sickness, dimly aware that she simply couldn't succumb to it here, on the main street of the town.

Jack and Neridah Gregg—together again! 'Oh, my God,' Kaarin moaned, suddenly wishing she hadn't burned the letter, wishing she could have read it, as if the reading could have prepared her for . . . this!

She plunged into the rear of the camper, slamming the door and drawing the curtains behind her before frantically pumping up a sink full of water and splashing it on her face and throat. Then she sat down on the narrow bunk and consciously tried to control her shuddering nerves.

So many questions, so much she wanted to know and yet feared to find out. But the sense of betrayal blotted out almost everything else, a betrayal that seemed to claw at her insides with talons of ice.

'And I . . . loved . . . you . . .' The words moaned forth in a dirge, repeated over and over as the tears rained down her face to drip unnoticed on the floor. She cried until there were no more tears, until her throat was raw.

The anger didn't take hold until she was about half-way back to the cabin, and when it did start, writhing up from inside in a steaming, frothing torrent, the intensity was so great that she had to pull off the road and stop for a moment until she had regained some semblance of control.

She took several deep breaths, looked dispassionately at the trembling of her fingers on the steering wheel, and then rammed the van into gear and tramped hard on the accelerator, surging back on to the road in a skidding, fish-tailing slide.

Damn him! The word reverberated through her skull like a curse as she flung the camper over the succession of narrow gravel tracks that led to the cabin. What she would do if Jack had arrived before her, she didn't know. And didn't really care, so long as somehow it allowed her the revenge her tortured heart demanded.

But when she arrived in the clearing, only the blue heeler was there to greet her, and the dog stayed only long enough to assure itself of Kaarin's identity before loping back to rejoin the pups.

Kaarin paid scant attention. Her primary concern was to gather together everything that was hers and get it properly loaded in the camper, ready for her own departure. Of course she couldn't leave until Jackson Collier returned; even in her vilest of tempers she wouldn't consider abandoning the dog, pups and chickens.

But she would cheerfully abandon Jack Collier, and once the van was loaded she began to plot just how to arrange it.

There was plenty of time for plotting; Jack didn't arrive that night, nor even the next. It wasn't until almost noon on Wednesday when his ancient utility finally came lumbering down the forest track to the cabin. And Kaarin was ready—more than ready—to greet him.

In the time since the newspaper picture had shaken

her to the very foundations of her beliefs, she had schemed and planned and plotted a host of vengeful words and actions for Jack's return, most of them so drastic that even her white-hot fury couldn't countenance them. And as his truck approached, his arm already raised in greeting, all her plots fled in a welter of confusion.

He was out of the truck as it slid to a halt and in three great steps he was before Kaarin on the verandah, his arms curling round her unprotesting body and his lips moving down to kiss her.

She met his kiss unresponsively, her lips like ice and her heart even chillier, but Jack seemed not to notice her coldness.

'Lord, I've missed you!' he murmured in her ear. 'I think I may never leave you again.'

She wanted to throw up. Hypocritical, lying devil! But she stubbornly summoned up a smile and nodded at his flattery. She would be nice; it wouldn't be for long.

'You look very tired,' she said, deliberately avoiding his eyes and praying he'd take it for shyness. 'Why don't you have a quick swim while I get lunch ready?'

'Not until you've seen your present,' he grinned. 'It is just fantastic! If I do say so myself.'

He turned back towards the truck, but Kaarin clutched at his arm and forestalled him.

'No,' she said, lowering her voice into a sultry, husky whisper that fairly screamed its falseness in her ears. 'First you have to get cleaned up and relax a bit. You look as if you've slept in that suit.'

'I have,' he grinned, rubbing at his stubbly chin with one palm. 'Oh, all right, I suppose we can save your present until after lunch, but frankly I'd rather you forgot about lunch and came for a swim *with* me.'

'I'll get some hot water ready so you can shave when you get back,' she said, her every nerve hustling him onward, out of the house and into the river. It took all of her endurance to keep from screaming at him, driving him away from her.

In the few minutes it took Jack to change into his familiar ragged shorts, Kaarin's mind ripped apart his loving, friendly, *two-faced*, *hypocritical* greeting, but she managed a warm, phoney smile as he trotted down the path towards the pool, calling back over his shoulder something about how much the pups had grown.

Obviously he hadn't noticed that she'd cleaned out every stitch of her clothing and every one of her possessions, including the typewriter, nor did he notice as she plucked the keys from his truck ignition and followed, slowly, to the crest of the hill.

Kaarin had already laid out the trappings of her plan. On the table inside the cabin, a single, still frozen steak and three eggs held a silent but unmistakable message. All that remained was to fling Jack's truck keys into the pool to ensure a lack of pursuit, and she would be inside her van and gone. Even when he found the keys, he would be held to the site by the same chains which had forced Kaarin herself to endure days of mental anguish—the dog and her pups and the chickens.

Even a proper louse like Jack wouldn't abandon his livestock to pursue a girl who obviously didn't want him, she reasoned, and reached the brow of the ridge with her hand already raised to throw the keys.

Only first she looked, then looked again in amazement. Where was Jack? The surface of the pool was smooth, unrippled; *his* rock was empty; and as her eyes scurried across the landscape they picked up no sign of the man himself.

Kaarin turned in panic, plunging back up the hillside in a straight line towards her camper. No matter that something had gone amiss, all that counted was for her to flee, now, before Jack returned from wherever he might be.

The keys in her hand rattled against the door of her van as she grabbed for the handle and yanked the door open. She looked down at them, then stared wildly around the clearing. Then, abruptly, she dropped them to the ground, scrambled into the driver's seat and reached for the ignition.

CHAPTER SEVEN

'SURELY you weren't planning on leaving without saying goodbye?' The voice from the rear of her camper fairly dripped with mockery and sarcasm. It was followed by a significant jingling sound as Jack shook the key-ring from the now-vacant ignition switch.

Kaarin sat in stunned silence. How could he? How had he known?

'Come on, love. You should know by now that I can read your mind,' he said, doing it yet again with an accuracy that terrified her.

Still she didn't answer. Waves of anger rushed in to displace her confusion, her inner hurting. To hell with him—she would say nothing.

Jack threw open the van's side door and stepped lightly to the ground, stooping instantly to pick up the key-ring she had dropped and then leaning down to stare owlishly at her through the window. Maddeningly, he raised her own key-ring and jingled it just out of reach.

'If you want these keys back you're going to have to explain things,' he cautioned, but the look in his eyes revealed that he considered the entire episode some kind of great, hilarious joke.

Kaarin turned her head away, showing him only her rigid shoulders and neck.

He laughed. Silently, but he laughed. She *knew* . . . she could *feel* the laughter. It ran like claws over her drum-tight nerves. But she didn't move.

'All right, suit yourself,' he growled after what seemed like hours. 'I'll be inside when you change your mind.'

She heard the sound of his retreating footsteps, but still she didn't turn her head. Not until her peripheral vision caught his shape as it moved towards the cabin porch. Then she lowered her head and shook it, sadly. Now what was she to do?

During the next hour her mind whirled and spun in a maelstrom of conflicting emotion. She loved Jack Collier . . . she hated him . . . he had betrayed her . . . he could explain . . . she should listen to him, let him explain . . . he would lie and cheat as he already had . . . On and on and on it went, until she was so totally unnerved and confused she could only sit, trembling, and stare straight ahead into the grey-green canopy of the surrounding scrub.

She could simply walk away! The thought struck her like a thunderclap, but even as she reached for the doorhandle her logic intervened. He was watching. He would find a way to stop her—physically, if all else failed, and deep inside Kaarin knew that she dared not allow him to touch her.

By three o'clock the inside of the van had become an oven. Kaarin still sat in the driver's seat, sweat pooling down beside her. Her blouse was saturated and the hair at her temples matted, but she didn't notice it that much.

She was hungry, and thirsty. But these too were only vague annoyances. The major annoyance was Jackson Collier, who stood leaning in casual comfort against the side of the van, his voice droning on.

'I honestly don't understand any of this, dear Kaarin,' he said for the third, fourth, fourteenth time. 'I know you can't be this upset just because I was a few days later than we expected. So it's something else. But what?

'Of course I've got a perfectly good excuse for being late, but you obviously aren't interested, so I won't bother you with it just now. Especially since I get the impression you wouldn't believe me anyway.

'Your "uncle" Bill sends his regards, by the way. Now that he's got most of the manuscript he's a much happier fellow than when you last saw him.

'Perhaps I'll nip into town tomorrow and give him a call. Maybe he knows what the hell's bugging you. But then he'd probably just start hassling me about the rest of the manuscript—unless of course you've already mailed it to him. Did you, Kaarin?

'I think you likely did; you've moved the van for some reason or other, although maybe it was just to arrange your quick exit.

'Aren't you getting hot in there? You *could* roll down the windows, you know. I'm not going to haul you out of there and paddle the answers out of you. Although I should.'

Kaarin stayed rigid, ignoring him with her eyes, which were blankly out of focus and staring. Mental fingers crushed against her ears, vainly trying to shut off the sound of his voice.

Deep inside her, other voices kept up a constant clamour, one pleading with her to be reasonable, to listen to Jack. Another screamed more loudly, 'You're winning!' She wasn't really listening to the inner voices, either, but was in a sort of self-induced trance, trying to escape everything . . . all of it.

'. . . knew you were stubborn, Kaarin, but I'd never thought of you as so . . . so totally unfair. I mean, anybody has a right to a hearing, especially when they don't even know what the charges are. What the hell am I supposed to have done?' His voice rose for the first time to reveal a hint of his growing frustration, and Kaarin thrilled inside at the revelation—and cried inside at this torture she was inflicting on the man she loved.

I hate you. She said it silently, without emphasis or feeling or even a glance in his direction. Ever since she had seen that newspaper, her mind had been filled with horrid, almost pornographic visions of Jack lying next to that Gregg woman, his lips touching her, his hands giving her the same ecstasy he'd provided for herself, his voice mouthing words of love.

Love! Empty words, false words. Emptiness inside her that was slowly filling with cold, frozen molten ice. She shivered.

'... suppose I *could* just let you go. I mean, after all, I'd know where to find you again when this great tempest in a teapot is over.'

Kaarin's heart gave a lurch of sudden hope, only to subside into the ice again at his next words.

'But I might never know when it was over. You're just prideful enough that you might decide never to tell me. The Kaarin I thought I knew wouldn't have, but you're not her. Damn it. *Damn it!* Why can't I get through to you?'

He left at five, returned at six with a tray of steaming food. Kaarin didn't even look, and finally he shook his head sadly, laid the tray on the grass beside the van, and walked back into the cabin.

A part of Kaarin's mind cried at the haggard look of him; he seemed to have lost weight, to have been without sleep for days. A triumphant voice inside chortled, 'You're winning. Winning!'

Darkness brought some relief from the inferno temperatures of the afternoon, but little else. Kaarin considered retiring to the rear of the camper to sleep, then slid into a restless slumber while she was thinking about it.

The scrambling clatter of a possum raiding her food tray woke her briefly, but when she looked towards the cabin and saw Jack's ghostly shape, watching, she blanked out her mind again and finally slept.

At dawn he came again, and she steeled herself for yet another show of resistance.

Eyes like blazing brown coals burned from a face that was pale with emotion. The muscles of his jaws were clenched into hard ropes beneath the stubble that blurred his jawline.

That much Kaarin saw as he approached the van, moving deliberately across the front so that she couldn't avoid seeing him.

She only heard his foot kicking the food tray into a spinning arc away from where he'd left it, but when his fingers touched the door handle her every sense stood on edge.

The door flew open and she shrank away from the fire-eyed figure that stooped inside, fingers outstretched to her like the claws of an animal. But he didn't touch her; instead the eyes softened and the great head shook wearily as he stared at her.

'You win.' The van keys tinkled as he threw them into her lap with a sneer of disgust and resignation, but before she could so much as pick them up, Jack had turned away, walking once again across in front of her. His broad shoulders were stooped and his walk held none of the usual spring, but he didn't look back even when he reached the verandah of the cabin and then stepped inside.

Kaarin's fumbling fingers dropped the keys once before she fitted the ignition key and got the engine running, but finally ... finally! ... she was free.

The van lurched into motion as she dumped the clutch and trod hard on the accelerator, ignorant of the engine's screams in the panic of her departure. She steered haphazardly along the narrow bush track with one eye on the road ahead and the other fixed on the rear-view mirror.

But by the time she'd reached the bitumen and swung south towards Ban Ban Springs, she knew there was no further need to look back. Jack wasn't following, and wouldn't. Or would he? Kaarin didn't dare risk being wrong; she knew she could never face Jack Collier in his present mood, so she didn't pause at Ban Ban Springs, but headed south on the Burnett Highway, driving fast enough so that her mind was forced to concentrate on the road ahead.

She swung left at Tansey to pick up the Wide Bay Highway at Kilkivan, then drove steadily until she reached the coastal Bruce Highway and Gympie, where exhaustion and hunger forced a halt.

It took all her control to force down the cardboard chicken and soggy chips that were brought to her in a restaurant chosen for its parking lot out of view of the main road, and she wondered at the odd looks she got from the waitress until she ventured to the dingy washroom and looked with wide-eyed horror into the mirror.

'I'm surprised they even let me in,' she muttered, digging out comb and make-up kit for a hasty but passable repair job.

She stayed that night in a small, tidy motel at Noosa Heads, at virtually the northern end of the Sunshine Coast. She had already decided not to follow the original plan of holidaying on the Gold Coast, south of Brisbane, but would instead wander her way southward from Brisbane in a lazy, relaxing trip that with luck would allow her to get her emotions under control before she reached Sydney and had to face Bill Cleaver.

As it turned out, the trip was anything but relaxing; it was a nightmare, except for the first day and a half. She spent that simply sleeping, eating and relaxing on the warm sands of Sunshine Beach, letting the hot sun and gentle sea breezes cleanse her of weariness. She washed her hair, stuffed herself on seafood delicacies and soaked up the sunshine through layers of sunscreen. She didn't think.

But once she had started driving south, through scenery of incomparable loveliness, some deep, subconscious portion of her mind seemed to spring forward, recreating the close, intimate haze of her association with Jack Collier.

She found herself remembering not his betrayal, but the touch of his hands, the textures of his hair and body, the gentle things and the incredible comfort of things shared.

Once she half turned in her seat, her mouth open to cry out her delight to him as she saw a tiny painted foal nudging lunch from his dam in a roadside paddock.

The fairytale castle at Bli Bli, replica of an eleventh-century Norman castle complete with moat and drawbridge, was spoiled for her because she kept turning subconsciously to point out things of interest to a companion who wasn't there. In the dungeon, she felt Jack's fingers touching her shoulder, but when she turned in confusion it was only another tourist with a question to ask of her.

From Nambour to Caboolture she drove with savage concentration, striving consciously to convince herself again how right she'd been to leave Mingo Crossing and how devilishly cruel Jack had been in leaving her to tend his chickens and feed his pups while he flew to a secret assignation with his high-society girl-friend.

But by the time she reached Brisbane, she knew that the holiday journey was a waste of time, and she thrust aside her tourist guides and forged ahead by the shortest and fastest route to Sydney. Sydney—not ... home, she realised, but at least a place where she could seek her 'uncle's' counsel and guidance.

'It's about time you showed up,' Bill Cleaver growled when she walked into the study where he was perusing a manuscript. There was none of his usual benign Buddha-like expression; he was angry and didn't mind showing it.

He slewed his chair around and glared up at Kaarin, in no way intimidated by her towering above him. 'Sit down,' he snapped. 'Sit down . . . and tell me just what the hell is going on between you and Jack Collier.'

Kaarin ignored the question.

'Did you get the rest of the manuscript I mailed?' she asked with a phoney but pleasant smile.

'A good try, but it's not going to work,' Bill snarled. 'Yes, I got the rest of the manuscript. Now sit down and tell me the answer to my original question.'

'I'm really very tired,' Kaarin replied evasively. 'Can't it wait until . . .' She waved one hand in a vague gesture that said nothing at all.

'It can wait until forever as far as I'm concerned,' he replied angrily. 'I mean, I've got nothing else to do but answer the phone forty times a day to have Jack threatening me with bodily injury because I won't force you to talk to him. Damn it, Kaarin—what the hell happened?'

'Nothing! Nothing happened at all,' she cried just as angrily.

His explosive retort was shocking not in its profanity, but because she had never . . . never heard him use the word before. It was also startlingly explicit.

At any other time it would have been more than sufficient to bring her into line, but she was no longer quite the pliant, easy-going country girl who had left this house only weeks before. Now her chin stiffened in stubborn defiance.

'Whatever happened is personal and none of your business—and don't you dare swear at me like that,' she flared. 'I won't have it!'

Bill Cleaver's eyebrows shot up in amazement, then he leaned back in his chair and—quite absurdly—beamed at her with the broadest smile she'd ever seen.

'Well, pardon me all to hell,' he said, shaking his head in obvious wonder. 'All right, we won't talk about it if that's what you want. Why don't you just trundle off to bed and get a good night's sleep? I know you've had a long and tiring drive and I'm sorry I hassled you.'

Kaarin stared down at him, the slight grin on her lips offset by the firm set of her eyes.

'We're not going to talk about it in the morning, either,' she warned.

He held both hands up in a gesture of dismay. 'Nothing was farther from my mind,' he lied, taking no trouble at all to try and disguise it.

'Promise?'

'Promise,' he agreed, and although Kaarin could see very well that he'd crossed his pudgy fingers to negate the promise, she kissed him fondly on the forehead and then went to her room for a shower and the relative comfort of her own familiar bed.

She got the first really good night's sleep she'd had since leaving Mingo Crossing, and woke with the dawn feeling fit enough even to cope with Bill Cleaver's interrogation. But when she had breakfast on the table and called him to join her, he fooled her by ignoring the Collier issue as if it didn't exist.

His opening gambit instead was, 'What are you planning for the rest of your holiday?'

Kaarin stammered in surprise and confusion. 'I . . . er . . . I hadn't really . . . thought much about it. Actually, I'd expected you'd want me back at work,' she replied.

'Do I take that to mean you've abandoned your original plan of getting away from the city?'

That was an unexpected question, especially for a girl who'd just gone to so much trouble to return to the safety of the city.

'I don't know,' Kaarin replied honestly enough. 'I just haven't thought that far ahead, to tell you the truth.'

'Hummph!' Bill Cleaver didn't sound greatly impressed, but nothing in his expression revealed any vivid concern. 'There'd be nothing for you to do in the office until Monday, at least,' he said finally. 'Why don't you hang about until then and see if you can get yourself together a bit better?'

'Why do I have the impression you don't want me back?' Kaarin asked lightly, hoping he wouldn't be able to pick up the vibes from the great sinking feeling inside her.

'No such thing,' he replied stoutly. 'No such thing at all. But you will remember that before you left on that ... er ... mission, you were trying to break it to me gently that you'd had the city up to here and really wanted to get away. Well, your ... er ... trip north has sort of added to that. I've got a replacement fairly well broken in now, and ... er ...'

'And ... er ... what?' Kaarin interrupted. 'You devious, cunning old rascal! You didn't expect me to come back from ... from ... up north at all, did you? Come on, 'fess up. Just how much arranging of my life did you eventually do with ... with Jackson Collier, anyway?'

'None! Not a single bit,' he denied vehemently. And then in a milder, more sober voice, 'although during his visit last week I got the distinct impression that you two had ... er ... rather arranged things fairly well yourselves.'

'Well, that's certainly not the impression I received,' Kaarin retorted. 'So if you don't mind, let's just drop the whole thing.'

'As you wish, as you wish,' her 'uncle' said placatingly. 'Although I would remind you that I didn't bring it up—you did.'

'Right! And I'm dropping it,' Kaarin snapped. 'Now, and for evermore. It would please me greatly if I never heard that man's name ever again.'

'Hmm. I suppose that means you wouldn't take kindly to my suggesting you proof-read his book for me.'

Kaarin gasped. 'I certainly would not! Really, Uncle Bill! Don't you think that's asking just a bit much? And for goodness' sake, why can't he proof read it himself? Is he helpless as well as ...' She couldn't finish.

Bill Cleaver raised both hands in a gesture of defeat. 'Not to the best of my knowledge, although he was still pretty weak when he left here,' he said, grabbing up his suit coat. 'And now, my child, I must adjourn to the saltmines. Consider the subject closed; forget I even mentioned it.'

He was gone before Kaarin could even think of a reply, much less think to question him about Jack Collier's having been *still pretty weak*.

During the day, a day in which she cleaned house, dusted, washed all her clothes and became abundantly, increasingly bored, the words kept recurring in her mind. It wasn't until dinner that night that she had any opportunity to query Bill about his remark.

Her choice of timing wasn't the best. Bill had obviously had a horrendous day and wasn't in any mood to play word games.

'Look, I don't remember exactly what I said this morning,' he complained. 'That was hours ago—years ago when you think of the day I've had. And what does it matter anyway? You've completely gone off the man. I thought you weren't going to discuss it any more.'

Kaarin had to accept that, and they both settled down to a dinner that should have been better than it was. She was in no mood to enjoy the meal, having spent more time preparing it than it deserved, but when Bill Cleaver pushed aside his pâté and muttered something Kaarin didn't hear, she caught him up on it.

'I said I may never eat pâté again,' he growled. 'Nothing personal, my dear. It's just that by having had the good fortune not to eat the pâté at that silly charity function, I saved myself the trouble of winding up in hospital with your friend Collier, not to mention Neridah Gregg and four dozen other guests.'

'Hospital? What are you talking about?' Kaarin cried, more concerned at the lack of information than at having her pâté so soundly rejected.

He looked at her as if she had gone off her head. 'What am I talking about? The food poisoning, of course. Goodness, Kaarin, didn't you talk to Collier at *all* when he got back? I mean, I realise you wouldn't have been getting the Sydney papers up there, but surely he told you about it?' He laughed ruefully. 'Helluva mess, it was. Fifty-three people in hospital, including Jack, Neridah Gregg and her fiancé and about half the city's top-drawer socialites. Jack got the biggest headlines, of course, being the guest of honour at the affair. And poor old Neridah was fit to be tied, of course, since it was she who arranged it all . . .'

He continued his monologue, but Kaarin was no longer listening. Her own mind was all tied up with the horrifying vision of her final confrontation with Jack Collier—her refusal to talk to him, and worst of all, her refusal to listen.

'Oh . . . my . . . God!' she whispered as the enormity of her error struck her. Then her stomach rebelled and she fled the dining room only just in time.

When she returned, white-faced and shaking, Bill Cleaver had adjourned to his study, poured out a large brandy for each of them, and was waiting for her with a look of long-suffering compassion on his cherubic face.

'Now I think we'd better discuss this matter of you and Jack Collier—whether you like it or not,' he decreed. 'That little performance, coupled with the telephone call I had today from Jack himself, has taken about the last of my patience.'

Kaarin took a gulp of the brandy and shuddered as it steamed down her throat to fire up the emptiness below. She shook her head wearily, oblivious to the tears in her eyes.

'You might as well hear it all,' she said. 'And then you can take me out and shoot me if I don't beat you to it.'

'Save the ridiculous histrionics,' he snapped. 'All I want to know is what two supposedly adult people could do that turns my favourite child into a nervous wreck and my star author into ... oh, come on, tell me!'

She did, slowly and with considerable difficulty as the words brought home just exactly how childish and immature she'd been.

'And that's ... that's it,' she concluded. 'Not a very impressive story, is it? Oh, Uncle Bill, what am I going to do?'

He shrugged. 'Personally, I'd say you've done just about enough. And stop that damned blubbering; it isn't helping. I'm not surprised Jack's so thoroughly disgusted with the whole affair; I share his feelings entirely, even though I realise he ought to be accepting at least some of the blame.'

'How could he possibly?' Kaarin cried. 'It was all my fault; he didn't do anything.'

'Precisely my point,' Bill Cleaver retorted. 'All it would have taken was the simplest of explanations in the very beginning, and I'd have other, more pleasant things to worry about. Ah well, at least the book got done.'

'That's a despicable thing to say!' Kaarin flared.

'Of course, but it stopped your blubbering, didn't it? And all the weeping and wailing in the world isn't going to fix this little muck-up.'

'What did ... Jack say when he rang today?' Kaarin had to force the question from her mouth, but once it was asked she waited eagerly for the answer.

'Well, it was an improvement over the other calls I've had since you left him—from my viewpoint,' Bill replied. 'But not from yours, I'm afraid.'

'Oh, please! Will you just tell me exactly what he said?' she pleaded.

'All right. Word for word?'

Kaarin nodded and he continued. 'He said, quote, is she back yet? unquote. I said, quote, yes, unquote. He said, quote, good, unquote. And then he hung up.'

'That's *all*?'

'Well, what would you expect after the silly damned stunt you pulled ... a forty-minute enquiry after your health? For your information, dear Kaarin, he gave up being solicitous after the second day. As of this moment, I'd say you've got a permanent reservation at the top of his ... black list.'

'And I deserve it, too, I know. But what am I going to *do*?' Kaarin could feel the tears lurking, ready to surge forth at the slightest provocation.

Bill reached over to pat her tenderly on the cheek. 'I think the best thing for you to do, right this minute, my dear, is sleep on it,' he said gently. 'It may seem like the end of the world, but it isn't, believe me.'

Easier said than done, Kaarin found during an endless, sleepless night that brought her to the breakfast table with huge dark rings under her eyes and legs that ached from pacing the floor of her room most of the night.

'I'm going to have to go back,' she said without preamble when Bill Cleaver entered the room.

'I suppose you will,' he replied without any great show of enthusiasm. 'But at the risk of sounding like a mercenary, money-grubbing capitalist, can I ask that you wait a day or two, get some *sleep*, and maybe even help your poor old uncle out by proofing Collier's damned book? At the very least wait until the day after tomorrow, when I'll have a full set of page proofs—God and the printers' union willing—and if nothing else you can take the proofs with you so that I can get this book into production.'

He paused, eyes glinting as he tried to read Kaarin's expression.

'Look,' he said then. 'At least it gives you a ready-made excuse for going, and if he turfs you out on your ear, which you mightily deserve, you can at least leave the proofs and let the trip count for something.'

Kaarin's eyes widened in disbelief. 'You're ... you're unbelievable! Is nothing as important to you as that damned book?'

To which her uncle replied with his most benevolent smile, 'Of course, my dear. You are. But I have the psychic ability to know that you'll work your problems out, sooner or later, to everyone's satisfaction. My bankers, on the other hand, have no such psychic ability concerning books that are already a month overdue. Also, I might point out, if it wasn't for that book you wouldn't have had the chance to get yourself into this unholy pickle.'

Suitably chastened, Kaarin gave in. 'All right,' she said. 'You're right, as usual. I'll come in with you today and tomorrow and correct the proofs, and I'll take them up to Jack when I go as well.' She gave a nervous little laugh that betrayed her inner misgivings. 'And even if he won't talk to me, I'm sure he'll check the proofs and get them back to you promptly.'

'Oh no!' Bill Cleaver's voice was adamant. 'Even if he doesn't talk to you, he will check the proofs and send them back with *you*. You will fly to Bundaberg; you will rent a car, go see Collier, and first—first—you will arrange for him to read the proofs and get them back here. After *that* you can worry about whether he talks to you or not. I want those proofs back here within four days of your leaving. Is that clear?'

'It's perfectly clear and it's perfectly ridiculous and you know it,' she replied. 'But I take your point, and I promise you that regardless of whether I can square myself with Jack or not, I'll make sure the proofs get back to you as soon as possible.'

'I have every confidence in you, my dear,' Bill Cleaver replied with a benign smile.

'Thanks very much; I just wish I had a tenth as much,' Kaarin responded with a rueful grin of her own. Then she shrugged. 'Still, I have to try and at least apologise, though after the way I've acted I wouldn't be surprised if he doesn't run me off with a shotgun.'

'It's far more likely he'll give you the spanking you so richly deserve,' said Bill. 'It sort of depends on whether he loves you as much as you love him.'

'It's that obvious?'

'Well, don't look so astonished. I couldn't imagine you being this upset if you didn't love him,' was the chuckled reply. 'And if it's any consolation, he appears to be equally upset, although I warn you it might just be because his pride has been severely kicked about. But a clever girl like you should be able to find a way around that.'

Kaarin had to laugh. 'We've already seen where being clever has got me,' she replied. 'I think maybe I'll just apologise for being a stupid, jealous child and take what comes after that on its own merits.'

'A wise decision. But don't neglect my earlier warning,' Bill grinned. 'If I were you I'd stuff a pillow in my jeans before I let Jack Collier get anywhere near me.'

'Being spanked is the least of my worries, Uncle Bill. And now I'd better go get ready to go to the office with you.'

'No, don't bother,' he said. 'I'll send the proofs back in a cab when I get to work and you can work here where there's less distractions. It'll be a couple of hours, so try and catch up on your sleep. You look like death warmed over.'

'You do such nice things for a girl's confidence,' Kaarin retorted, but privately she agreed with him, and once Bill Cleaver had left for his office she did try and rest until the cab arrived with the proofs.

Poring over the neat galleys was both easier and more difficult than she'd anticipated, however. The haste of the typesetting had resulted in more errors than usual, and correcting them was the easy part.

The difficulty was in the pangs of nostalgia and memory that plagued Kaarin throughout her task. During the two days of proof-reading, she kept having to yank her mind away from her Utopia at Mingo Crossing and back to the task at hand.

She practically knew the book by heart, but even so, the scenes word-painted by Jack Collier kept conjuring up equally vivid memories of his lovemaking, his touch, his tenderness. Followed by harsher recollections of her own jealous folly and the consequences to come.

'You've just got to let me explain,' she muttered to herself at one point. 'Even if you never speak to me again afterwards.'

Then she shook her head angrily. *That* was a thought she preferred not to contemplate further. Jack would *have* to let her explain, she thought. But much as she loved him, and much as she believed he might love her in return, there was the continuing, horrible fear that she'd pushed him too far, that the magic could never be regained.

CHAPTER EIGHT

'HE said *what?*' Kaarin's mind whirled in momentary confusion. Her uncle's blatant announcement when he sat down to dinner had thrown all her plans for a loop, and she had difficulty assimilating it all.

'He said there was no sense sending up the proofs because he was too busy to bother, especially since you'd already done the proof-reading. I told him that, of course.'

'And I suppose you also told him it was I who'd be bringing the proofs up, which is why he's decided not to bother.' Kaarin could just visualise Jack's reaction to that situation.

'I did no such thing,' Bill Cleaver replied. 'He phoned specifically to ask about the proofs and all I said was that you'd already read them and that I'd be sending them up for his personal check tomorrow. His reaction was exactly what I've told you. He said that if you'd read the proofs and corrected them it would be silly to waste time sending them to him.'

He paused then and took a sip of his wine. 'Frankly, I'd have expected you to be pleased at the show of confidence. Although it does sort of blow your excuse for going up there, doesn't it?'

'Doesn't it just?' Kaarin replied ruefully. 'But it doesn't change anything. I've still got to go; this just makes it a bit trickier, that's all.'

'I suppose it would be a waste of time pointing out the difference between him having confidence in your professional abilities and wanting you showing up on his doorstep unannounced.'

'It would,' she replied firmly. 'Nor do I especially expect a rousing welcome. But I just have to try and explain, or at least apologise for running out on him before. And I can think of no other way to do that, unless you'd rather I wait until his next visit here, which could be months from now.'

'Longer than that, I should imagine,' Bill Cleaver replied dryly. 'I got the distinct impression that he'll be doing no more writing—or socialising—until he gets that house finished.'

'Right, then. And since you've already half admitted there's no longer a place for me in your office ... no, don't bother to deny it, I understand ... then I might as well go back up there, straighten this thing out as best I can, and then see about finding a job somewhere,' she said.

She would, too. Perhaps in Bundaberg, or even Gayndah, which she'd quite liked and which, to be honest, was close enough to Jack Collier's base that she might at least see him from time to time.

It all sounded terribly plausible, and she even managed, during the two-day drive north, to almost convince herself it was possible. But when she woke up with the sun in the motel at Ban Ban Springs, with her confrontation with Jack only hours away, reality crept in with frightening second thoughts.

Outside in her elderly Mini were all her worldly possessions, mostly clothes and some favourite books. She had enough money to subsist for a month or two while seeking a job, and the qualifications to find one with relative ease. But none of these things could aid her in facing up to Jack's predictable scorn and contempt, although face them she must.

Her knuckles were white on the steering wheel and tension was a writhing, growing caterpillar in her stomach when she finally nosed the Mini cautiously into the clearing and up to the sagging porch of the cabin. She flinched, first with alarm and then with smiling amusement, as the blue heeler bitch charged over the brow of the hill, barking with alarm and echoed by the four miniatures of herself that followed.

'Hello, old girl,' said Kaarin, stepping out of the car to the immediate destruction of her hose as the four pups tried to clamber up her legs.

The old dog's growls changed to whines of affection with her first sniff of Kaarin, but instead of sitting to have her ears scratched she immediately turned back towards the building site, shaking her head and whining in an unmistakable plea for Kaarin to follow.

Kaarin followed, moving cautiously over the uneven ground in her high-heeled shoes, but as she reached the brow of the hill and stared down in horrified alarm, the sight before her destroyed all caution. She plunged down the hill, oblivious to her own safety in her concern for what lay below.

The crumpled figure of Jack Collier, pinned to the ground by a huge beam that had obviously fallen when he had been trying to raise it, was terrifying enough; the blood that pooled around his head so frightened Kaarin that she could think only, for one horrible instant, that he had killed himself.

Around her, the world seemed to swim in a haze of blurred lights, whirling and dancing until she shook off the shock and knelt beside him. He was still breathing, but his pulse was erratic when she took up his wrist to check.

And the blood! She had to pause yet again to summon mental control for her heaving stomach before she tore a handful of tissues from her handbag and began to sponge away the blood so that she could see how badly he was hurt.

'Scalp wounds always bleed a great deal, even minor ones,' she said to herself, repeating the words over and over in a litany of despair as another part of her mind began making plans.

How long had he been here? And how serious was

the injury that had already raised an enormous lump around the long gash at his crown?

Kaarin's mind spun through half-forgotten first-aid rules. Did she dare to move him? 'Do I dare *not* move him?' she whispered aloud.

It would take her an hour to get help, short of driving out to stop somebody on the highway. And even that was too long a chance ... far too long. As the tissues gradually sponged away the blood, she could see that the scalp was slashed in a long, ragged cut. But it didn't appear too deep. Concussion or serious brain damage was the great fear, and in this isolated circumstance moving him was a justifiable risk.

She checked his pulse and breathing once more before rising to study the system of pullies and tripods he'd been using to raise the heavy rafters. She couldn't possibly move the beam that pinned him down without some mechanical aid, and—thank God—she quickly recognised how it might be done.

The beam lay across his back and shoulders, one end already dug into the ground beyond his feet and the other projecting a foot or so in front of him. To move it would require her to first shift one of the enormous tripods he had rigged, but after considerable straining she got the thing in place by shifting one leg at a time. It seemed to take forever.

The hardest part was securing the rope; the best place for doing so was smeared with blood and hair, obviously where it had struck him on the head in falling.

She had to force herself to slow down, to approach the problem carefully, cautiously. A mistake would mean even further injury, and she simply couldn't face that possibility. Even with the advantage of the block and tackle, she couldn't afford the slightest mistake, and it took every ounce of her strength to heave on the rope until the beam was lifted only a few inches.

Quickly now! She threw several half-hitches around one leg of the tripod, then darted in to grab Jack's arm and shoulder, dragging him inch by horrifying inch from under the precarious balance of the beam. When the cloth of his shorts caught, making the beam wiggle as it hovered menacingly over his thigh, she cried out in her terror, and fear gave her the extra strength then to free the cloth and swivel him around until the threat was nullified.

But now what? She knew it would be impossible to carry him, or even to drag him up the steep slope to where the vehicles were. And to risk bringing one down would be sheer folly; she might never get it back up the slope.

Her mind raced through the possibilities, her eyes searching the area for anything that might help. But it was memory that paid off in the end. Kicking off her clumsy shoes, she lurched her way back up the hill, only to return with the long section of roofing iron she'd remembered seeing stacked by the hen-run.

Laying it beside Jack's unconscious form, she grabbed up a hammer and several of the strong spikes she found lying about, and smashed the spikes through the iron.

They would hold. They'd have to hold, she thought, securing one end of the longest rope she could find to the spikes and then hammering them over to clinch it down.

Rolling Jack on to the makeshift sledge took all of her strength, but she managed it finally and then secured his wrists to the haul rope with several short pieces of lighter cord she found coiled by a stack of mud bricks.

It was time-consuming and frustrating beyond belief to then have to link one rope with another, then with a third and a fourth, until finally she had enough pieces joined to reach over the crest of the hill. She drove her

Mini as close as she dared, secured the rope to the undercarriage, and uttered a devout prayer as she thrust the little car into reverse and began backing away, inching the roofing iron and its burden slowly up the hill.

When she saw the iron come over the crest and begin bumping its way over the more level ground towards the cabin, she cried out her relief that Jack hadn't somehow slipped off, then she turned her mind to the most complicated part of her problem.

She couldn't possibly lift him into the Mini without causing further injury; he was much too heavy and too tall as well. It would have to be his old utility, but how to get him loaded?

There was only one answer, risky in the extreme but possible. Struggling for control of her shaking legs, she manoeuvred the utility into position, dropped the tailgate and brought up several short planks from below.

It took time, but finally she had the roofing iron in position at the bottom of the ramp and the rope slung straight over the cab of the utility and down to the front of the Mini. Not daring to think of the consequences should she fail, Kaarin started the car and backed slowly away, praying through clenched teeth as the slack was taken up and the rope stretched taut ahead of her.

The cab of the truck blocked her vision, and she could only inch backwards, rearing high in her seat to try and see what she was accomplishing. She went as far as she dared, then stopped the little car in gear and slid out to run behind the utility and check her progress.

Almost perfect; Jack was balanced lightly on the lip of the utility box. Dared she use the car again, or was it safer to try and shove the roofing iron from behind?

She tried that first, and breathed a heartfelt grunt of relief as it squealed grudgingly forward and then settled with a creak inside the bed of the truck.

The rest was much easier. She brought out every piece of bedding she could find in the cabin and moulded it into a pad before rolling Jack off the iron and on to the makeshift mattress. She got fresh, clean water and cloths and bathed the scalp wound that persisted in bleeding, though not as badly as before.

There was no way to secure him; she'd have to drive with great care to keep him from rolling around, but at least his breathing was regular now. The erratic pulse worried her.

It took more than an hour, an hour in which she drove as if transporting the most fragile of glassware, but finally, incredibly, the outskirts of Gayndah hove into view.

Kaarin screamed at the first person she saw, a man who recoiled in shock at the sight of her blood-smeared face and dress, but recovered within seconds to jump into the truck beside her and direct her to the hospital.

She managed to recount what she knew of the accident, told the authorities who Jack was and answered what questions she could, but the trembling of her body wouldn't stop and when a doctor suggested an injection for her own shock, she meekly accepted it after being assured over and over that Jack was being cared for.

Then there was the nightmare of waiting, not fully asleep or awake in a tiny room where they had taken her while someone cleaned up her face and blood-smeared hands, and took away her dress to try and clean it as well. She was sitting up in the bed, uncomfortable in the hospital smock, when an elderly, kindly-looking doctor came in to her.

'Well, that was quite a rescue operation,' he said. 'No, don't get up. I think you've used up quite enough energy for one day.'

'Is he . . .?'

'He'll be all right, thanks to you. The cut on his head is nowhere near as bad as it looked, but the tests show a slight concussion and some cuts and bruises down his back. With any luck he'll be out of here in a week.'

'Can . . . can I see him?'

He looked doubtful, and her eyes widened with fresh alarm. 'Well, not just now. I've given him a shot that will keep him asleep for a fair bit. And . . . you're not family or anything?'

'I'm . . . I'm his fiancée,' Kaarin replied as firmly as she could manage it. She wouldn't—couldn't—let them refuse to let her see him. She just couldn't!

The doctor smiled. 'Well, he's a damned lucky man,' he replied. 'Now, Miss Amos, I'd like you to try and sleep for a few hours, if you can. There'll be no need to keep you here overnight, but if you like I can try and make some arrangement . . .'

'No,' she replied. 'I'll have to go back to . . . to our property. There are animals to care for. But . . . but I'll be able to see him first?'

'Of course. And if you come in tomorrow you can spend all the time with him you like. He'll be awake then and able to appreciate it. Now try and rest. Here, I'll give you this one pill, nothing to worry about, it'll only help you to sleep.'

Kaarin took the pill obligingly. It would be all right now. They'd let her see Jack, and he was going to recover. She was smiling to herself when the pill took effect and she drifted into sleep.

'We weren't able to get all the stains out, I'm afraid,' said the young ward aide when Kaarin awoke to find her hanging up the dress in the room's small wardrobe.

'It doesn't matter,' Kaarin replied, her head filled with cotton wool and her mouth dry and tasting awful. 'Can I see Jack now, please?'

'I'll check with the doctor while you tidy up,' smiled the girl. 'I mean, you wouldn't want him to see you looking quite like you do, if you don't mind me saying so.'

When Kaarin looked at herself a few minutes later in the mirror, she understood the girl's point. But a few minutes' work with borrowed comb and make-up fixed that, except for the dress.

'He won't wake up, I shouldn't think, so don't let the dress worry you,' said the doctor when he came to take her into Jack's room. 'And I'll only leave you for a few minutes; he'll be better without any disturbances.'

The unspoken message was clear enough. 'I won't do anything to disturb him,' Kaarin smiled. 'I'm all right now, really, and I do understand.'

But when she saw Jack's pale face, seemingly as white as the bandage on his head, her stomach flip-flopped and her knees almost collapsed beneath her. He looked so ... so ... 'Is he all right?' she whispered, lowering herself to a bedside chair and reaching out to catch up his hand in her own.

'He'll be fine,' the doctor assured her. 'Provided, of course, he gets enough rest and doesn't start climbing ladders or some such silly thing the minute you get him home.'

'There'll be none of that, I can assure you,' she replied, never taking her eyes from Jack's pale, shockingly white face.

When the doctor returned after about fifteen minutes, she was in exactly the same position, and although she'd refrained from trying to talk to the unconscious man whose hand she still held, her thoughts had more than clarified her love for him.

You'll be all right. You *must* be all right, she thought over and over. I don't care if we never get things squared away between us; I don't care if you never speak to me again, just get better and get out of this place and . . . maybe some day . . .

The enforced rest during the morning at the hospital made it difficult for Kaarin to settle down when she'd returned to the emptiness of the cabin that afternoon. She filled the time by cleaning up, washing dishes, sponging out the blankets and sheets on which Jack had ridden to the hospital. And worrying.

She cooked herself a meal, then found herself barely able to eat it. The pups enjoyed what she left. At dusk she wandered down to the swimming hole and forced herself to churn back and forth, stretching her muscles and doing nothing at all to clear her mind.

It was warm enough, thank goodness, that she didn't need any blankets on the daybed, and she slept surprisingly well, to waken at dawn to the growling of the pups as they romped on the porch.

Kaarin dressed casually in the pale blue sundress she knew Jack had once admired, but she took extra care with her make-up to extinguish the smudges beneath her eyes and the paleness of her cheeks.

By the time she reached Gayndah, this time in the Mini, hunger was a gnawing pain inside her that rivalled the other tensions, so she stopped first downtown and choked down a hearty breakfast.

It was no comfort to be greeted at the hospital as something of a heroine. Every time one of the nurses or ward aides mentioned her *fiancé*, Kaarin's heart lurched with apprehension. Was Jack awake? And—oh God, what would *his* reaction have been to being told of his fiancée?

Stark terror halted her at the door to his room, her legs immobilised as her mind swayed towards the urge to just run . . . to get away.

'He's much better today, and I know he's looking forward so much to seeing you,' the nurse with her said kindly. She almost pushed Kaarin into the room in her eagerness to be a witness to the romantic reunion she expected.

Inside the door, Kaarin's legs almost failed her again as she looked down to meet dark brown eyes that roved lingeringly over her face. Jack looked worse, if anything, than he had the night before. A bruise had darkened on his forehead and another was swollen slightly on one cheekbone.

But he was alive, and awake. His lips parted in a painful grin as Kaarin stood rooted just inside the room.

She opened her mouth to speak, but the words stalled in her throat. Meeting his eyes wasn't difficult, until she caught the gleam of hidden mockery there.

'Well, come and give us a kiss,' he croaked. 'It's okay; I'm not broken or anything, just banged up a bit.'

Kaarin moved forward like a broken puppet, feeling herself totally without co-ordination but compelled by his dark eyes to reach the bedside, kneel and offer her lips.

But the token kiss she'd subconsciously planned took on startling new dimensions as his mouth closed over hers, a hand lifted to steady her as he held her to him, lips searing against her own in a kiss that would be the talk of the hospital for weeks.

'I'll ... er ... I'll just leave you two alone now,' said the wide-eyed nurse after Jack had finally released Kaarin. And she fled the room precipitately, leaving no room for doubt about her intention of telling everyone about the reunion.

'I think we've just made her day,' Jack chuckled, slowly releasing Kaarin until she had fumbled her way on to the chair by his bed. 'Want to do it again, just for us?'

She shook her head, almost in a panic at the way her body had so readily succumbed to his touch. She was all aflutter inside, and if he touched her again she feared she would melt.

'Coward!' he chuckled. 'Okay, sit there where I can't get at you, and tell me what it's like to be a heroine. From everything I've heard you arrived just in the nick of time, but I'd sure like chapter and verse on how you managed to get me here.'

'It wasn't . . . exactly easy,' she said. 'And . . . oh, it doesn't matter anyway. Are you all right? That's what's important.'

'Well, of course I'm all right, except that my head hurts like hell,' he said. He reached up to gingerly finger the bandage at his crown. 'Must have got a helluva whack, although of course I don't remember it. Like a few other things I could mention.'

Kaarin met his eyes, suddenly shy of the devils that lurked beyond the pain.

'I . . . I can explain . . .' she faltered, but was interrupted.

'I'm sure you can,' he cut in. 'In fact it ought to be a truly fascinating explanation, considering the giant step between your mood last time I saw you and our . . . rather sudden engagement.'

'I was . . . afraid they wouldn't let me in to see you, otherwise,' she whispered, not able to look at him now and all too aware of the flush that rose from her breast to colour throat and cheeks.

'Well, now isn't the time to talk about it,' he exclaimed with sudden weariness, and Kaarin looked up to find his eyes filled with pain.

'Go see if you can get a nurse to bring me another painkiller,' he grated, flinching as if the words hurt him. 'And then you might check with the doctor and find out how long I'm going to have to be here.'

'You'll be here until I say you can leave,' came a dry voice from the doorway, and Kaarin sighed with relief as the doctor stepped into the room.

'Perhaps you'd like to wait outside and I'll see you in a few minutes, my dear,' he said, firmly but gently escorting her out of the room. 'You can see him again this afternoon, but now I think a little sleep is more important.'

She paced the waiting room floor in increasing apprehension, oblivious to the comforting remarks of various passing nurses, until he finally joined her, a broad smile on his face.

'Stubborn man you've agreed to marry,' he chuckled. 'Damned fool tried to tell me he wants to go home—now! Utter silliness, of course. I want him here at least until tomorrow afternoon, just in case. And if there are no complications you can have him then and welcome, although he'll have to come back in a week or so to have the stitches out.'

Kaarin's gasp of relief only made him grin the wider.

'Don't look so grateful. I can tell without asking that he'll be a handful to look after. You'll want to have a firm hand with him, I warn you.'

'I'm sure I'll be able to manage,' Kaarin replied, her thoughts so full of happiness that she would have promised anything. The doctor wasn't so easily pacified.

'I just wish I could be as sure,' he cautioned. 'If I were you I'd start whipping him into shape now, while he's still not quite up to scratch. See that you do it, my dear, or I'll have to keep him here for a week in his own best interests.'

'Maybe . . . maybe that's what you should do,' she said with growing uncertainty. 'I mean, if that's what's best . . .'

'It's not, really. Half my nurses are already in love with him, not that I imagine you'll have to take that too seriously, and frankly I can't spare the room, either. He'll do just as well at home, provided you can force him to take things easy for a week or so.'

He grinned then at her obvious concern. 'Don't look so worried. I'll put the fear of God into him for you before I let him go.'

'And so will I,' she promised. 'So . . . will . . . I.'

It was easier than she would have thought. In the questionable privacy of the hospital she could easily refuse to discuss their 'engagement', and Jack himself refused to allow any talk involving her precipitate departure after his Sydney trip.

And when, finally, she was allowed to help him into the Mini's passenger seat for what she promised the doctor would be a 'slow and sedate' journey back to the property, he insisted that she fill the time by recounting in total detail her exploits in rescuing him and getting him to hospital.

'That's astounding,' he said when she had finally told the tale to his satisfaction. 'I'd have expected you to be resourceful, but really, you outdid yourself on that one.'

'It's hardly an exercise I'd like to repeat,' Kaarin replied. 'So just see that you obey the doctor's orders—which, I might remind you—includes obeying *my* orders.'

'Oh, but of course.' He said it so obviously tongue-in-cheek that she had to look across to see if he was also crossing his fingers and laughing. It was somewhat surprising to find him doing neither.

'Well, I mean, after all, you *are* my fiancée,' he said in mock seriousness, whereupon his grin escaped and Kaarin couldn't help but match it.

'I don't think we have to dwell on that,' she said. 'I've already explained why I said it, and it's served its purpose now.'

'You mean you aren't going to hold me to it? That's a bit weak. I mean, you've got witnesses and everything. Think of the breach of promise suit you could cop, especially after having saved my life. Why, you'd be guaranteed headlines all over the...'

'Oh, stop it!' Kaarin snapped, yanking the little car around a twist in the road so quickly that Jack's entire body snapped against the seat belt.

A gasp of pain escaped him, and she was immediately sorry, but he brushed aside her apology. 'My fault,' he growled. 'Hate hospitals ... always have. And staying in one with a perpetual headache hasn't done anything for my sense of humour.'

'I won't argue that,' she replied grimly. And then, in a brighter tone, 'It hasn't helped mine either, I'm afraid.'

'Ah well, we can be miserable together, then,' he grinned. 'Or are you just going to drop me at the cabin and disappear again?'

'Don't be daft,' she snapped. 'Although if you're going to act like this it's only what you deserve. The trouble is you're not safe to leave alone. I'm surprised you didn't do yourself an injury long before this.'

'Actually, I have,' he admitted with a wry grin. 'Only luckily they weren't serious enough to cause any problems. Sometimes I reckon that as a carpenter I make a good plumber.'

'Well, for the next week, at least, you're going to be neither. I want your promise on that,' she said, slowing in front of the cabin as the bitch and her blue horde swarmed out to meet them.

Jack grudgingly promised, then continued, 'But it's going to make for a boring week. Why the hell didn't you tell them you were my wife? Then we could have at least spent the week on a honeymoon.'

Kaarin's knees turned to water and she felt her heart lurch at the implications of his suggestion. But she tried, and managed, to create a light, breezy and totally negative response.

'In your condition? I'd be a widow before it was

over,' she laughed, hoping he couldn't sense the yearning inside her.

Jack eased himself out of the tiny car, knelt down to fondle the leaping, writhing pack of puppies, and then straightened up slowly with a painful twist of his neck. 'You're probably right, more's the pity,' he grunted. 'I guess I'll just have to settle for the engagement until I've recovered.'

Once inside the cabin, he meekly accepted Kaarin's order to lie down and rest while she prepared the evening meal, and before she even had the potatoes peeled he was fast asleep on his bed in the sleep-out with a puppy under each arm and the other two snuggled round his feet.

Her first reaction was to shoo them away, but after deciding that would only waken Jack unnecessarily, she slipped away and got her camera, taking several excellent pictures of the scene.

He was slightly more rested-looking when the meal was ready, but flatly rejected Kaarin's tentative approaches to making the apologies she'd originally come to make.

'I don't want to discuss that, and I'm sick, so you have to do what I want,' he said in deliberately childish tones. 'I don't know why you want to talk about that anyway; being engaged is far more fun. I've never tried it before. Have you?'

Her admission that no, she had never been engaged, did nothing to ease the feeling she had that he was toying with her, deliberately mocking her and having a good laugh at her expense.

Nor did he deny it when she finally accused him directly and demanded that he stop.

'I don't see why I should; it was your idea,' he said haughtily. 'Actually, we probably wouldn't make a bad team. With your cooking and typing and my great literary talents . . .'

'Stop that! Stop it right now or I'm leaving,' she shouted, leaping to her feet and nearly overturning the table in the process.

Jack leaned back in his chair, totally complacent. 'That's the only trouble with you,' he said. 'You always want to run away from everything. If you weren't so ready to run it wouldn't be nearly so easy to pick on you.' And he grinned maliciously. 'I liked you better when you first got here and every time I bugged you, you snapped back twice as hard. I shouldn't have started being nice to you, it's turned you into a little bit of a coward.'

Kaarin stood there with her mouth open. She didn't believe it . . . couldn't believe it. Her—a coward!

Well, all right for you, Jack Collier, she thought. You asked for it, and by God you'll get exactly what you asked for.

'You can afford to talk big,' she snarled, and most of the snarl was no put-on. 'You're pretty safe with your head cracked open and guaranteed invalid status. I suppose next you'll be telling me to take off my glasses and fight like a man. Well, that's it, mate. That is damned well *it*! I came out here to apologise to you for something I did that deserved an apology, but all I get for my trouble is abuse and more abuse. So forget it, I'll stay here and play nursemaid until I'm convinced you're well enough to leave alone, and then I'll be gone so quick it'll make your head spin.

'And let me tell you this, *Mr* Collier—I *won't* be running. I'll just be walking—or crawling, if I must. It couldn't matter less so long as it gets me away from the most conceited, arrogant, ignorant, chauvinistic pig of a man I've ever met!

'And just one more smart crack out of you and I'll give you a matching smack on the other side of your head, you self-righteous prig! Now why don't you get your butt out of that chair and do the dishes—or are you too *sick* for that? *I'm* going for a swim—alone!'

And she flounced out of the cabin before he had any chance at all to retaliate, fleeing down the track to the pool and hoping she'd get there before the tears came.

CHAPTER NINE

'COME on, lazybones. You can't spend the rest of your life in bed. Get up or I'll send the pups in to chew on your toes.'

The words seemed strange in the context of the rather erotic dream Kaarin was having, but the voice was right, and so was the touch of Jack's lips on her own. Without thinking, she lifted her arms round his neck, only to have him pull away sharply, thrusting her rudely into total wakefulness.

'Hey! None of that so early in the morning,' he growled with mock anger. 'Besides, I'm still sick. *And* starving. Get up and cook me some breakfast, woman.'

'After *that* rude awakening? You can cook your own breakfast and bring me mine in bed,' Kaarin replied tartly.

She wasn't entirely sure how he'd react to this kind of thing, especially after having returned from her swim the evening before to find the dishes washed, but Jack already sound asleep in his bed with pups everywhere round him.

'I don't have time to cook; I've work to do,' he replied. 'You can't expect me to cater to your whims and build my house at the same time.'

Work! Kaarin spun out of the narrow daybed, oblivious to her exposure beneath the flimsy nightgown she'd worn to bed.

'You're doing nothing of the kind,' she cried angrily. 'Damn you, Jack Collier, are you completely insane? Don't you dare even think of working on that house for at least a week. That's what the doctor said, and you promised ... Now go and sit down while I get breakfast—and don't you so much as leave ...'

Kaarin broke off at the sight of Jack slowly subsiding into a kitchen chair, an enormous grin on his face as he leaned back with his hands behind his head.

'Ah, that's more like it,' he sighed. 'Nothing like a bit of excitement to get a lazy woman out of bed in the morning.'

'You ... you ... You *tricked* me! You dirty rotten swine!' Kaarin shouted, half inclined to laugh with him, but with her jangled nerves so confused she was afraid she'd burst out crying instead.

'Got you out of bed, didn't it?' he replied blandly. 'And it was either that or climb in there with you. Would you have preferred that?'

'No, I certainly would not,' she replied, though with somewhat less vigour than her earlier protestation. Suddenly she was all too conscious of how revealing her nightgown could be, and she fled to the bathroom for her robe.

When she returned, he hadn't moved, but the laughter was even stronger in his dark eyes. 'Ah, modesty,' he sighed. 'You know, if you keep this up we'll have to bring in a chaperone.'

'If you'd just remember you're supposed to be a gentleman, there'd be no need at all,' Kaarin replied, turning away to begin making the coffee. Damn the man, she thought. Didn't he know that his suggestiveness was totally demoralising her? All he had to do was touch her and her control fled as quickly as her desires flared up inside her.

'A gentleman is the last thing I'd claim to being,' Jack laughed. 'What I am, dear girl, is a survivor, which is an entirely different thing.'

'I'm sure it is,' Kaarin retorted. 'And from the look of your head, you'd have done better to try being a gentleman.'

'Well done! A good night's sleep has improved your mettle considerably.' Jack chuckled at the scornful glare she threw him over her shoulder. 'But what I want to know is what we're going to do today.'

'*You're* going to rest.' Her flat tones should have killed any argument, but he only laughed behind her back.

'Of course I'm going to rest, but what am I going to do while I'm resting?' he continued. 'Or, more to the point, what are you going to allow me to do?'

'Read a book.' They were the first words that came into her head.

'Boring!' His reply was equally brusque.

'Sleep.' Two could play this game, she thought.

'After thirteen hours' sleep last night? Have a heart!'

'Well, what do you want to do, then?' she almost shrieked, not bothering to hide her own exasperation.

'I want to go to Bundaberg.'

'No!' The denial emerged even as she thought it; the idea of his driving two hours each way was unthinkable.

'You can drive me. That way I could rest during the trip. Hell, it isn't all that far.'

'And what are you going to do when we get there ... sit in the car and watch the traffic? You're in no shape to be roaming the streets.'

'We could go for lunch. Think about that, you wouldn't have to cook.'

'It would be easier to cook,' she retorted. 'Why do you want to go to Bundaberg anyway?'

'Oh, just a couple of things I want to attend to. You know ... business.' He was too, too casual.

'I don't trust you,' she replied, her eyes confirming it. 'You're plotting something, which means you've got something in mind you know I'm not going to like.'

'Untrue! And stop trying to read my mind. In the first place it's my trick, not yours. And in the second it's a gambit for married ladies; you're only engaged.'

'I am no such thing! And if you don't stop teasing

me about it, I'll . . .'

'You'll do nothing, because there's nothing you can do,' he laughed. 'It was your idea and now you're stuck with it.'

'In a pig's eye.'

'If you say so, dear affianced,' he laughed—then ducked when she swung the frying pan towards his head in a gesture that wasn't as phoney as it looked.

'Careful!' he warned. 'You'd have a helluva time explaining it at the hospital if you did hit me.'

'I wouldn't bother explaining. I'd just dump you into the river and let the fish have you,' she snapped, then grinned despite herself.

'You're terribly vicious. I'm not sure I dare allow you to trim my hair around this stupid bandage,' Jack replied. 'But try anyway, will you. After breakfast, of course.' And, to her relief, he turned the conversation to lighter, less personal subjects, while they ate.

The scalp wound was healing nicely, and Kaarin was able to replace the dressing with a much smaller one, although even that was terribly conspicuous. Perhaps more so because Jack insisted on changing into what he called *civilised* clothes for the journey to town.

And even with the still-dark bruising on his face and the innocuous white of the bandage, he looked startlingly tanned and healthy in a light cotton-duck safari suit and rope-soled sandals.

Kaarin put on a tidy pink halter-necked sundress that showed off her tan to good advantage and would be cool throughout the day, but threw a light sweater into the car in case they were late returning.

They reached Bundaberg in the Mini just before noon, after a drive in which Jack refrained from serious teasing and instead spoke to Kaarin in very sensible terms about his work, her work, and his progress on the house prior to the accident.

Once into the downtown shopping area, he insisted

she park near a telephone booth and wait while he made a series of calls, then directed her to park near the Chinese restaurant they'd missed on that long-ago visit she still remembered so vividly.

During a huge luncheon of Mongolian lamb, roast duckling with orange sauce, a specially-made chow mein and various smaller dishes of assorted delicacies, he seemed unusually quiet, and Kaarin began to worry about his health.

'No . . . I'm fine,' he replied instantly at her hesitant query. 'Just thinking, that's all. Have you got any really close friends? Besides me, I mean.'

Kaarin was struck dumb by the disclosure. She loved Jack, more than anything in the world. But she hadn't consciously considered their relationship in terms of friendship. She thought of querying his remark, but then decided it was better not to. Instead she replied with direct honesty.

'Only Uncle Bill . . . Bill Cleaver. But as you know, he isn't really my uncle . . .'

'I know that,' he interrupted. 'Okay, here's the problem. The very best friend I have in the world happens to be here in Bundaberg and I want to surprise that person—today. But I need your help.'

Kaarin looked at him sceptically. 'I knew you were plotting something,' she said. 'And the way your mind works I don't think I should help you at all. It's probably the most horrid kind of surprise . . . a practical joke or something.'

'I swear to you that it isn't, but I can't explain,' he said. 'All I can say is that it's the most pleasant surprise I can possibly imagine for the person involved, because it will clear up a whole host of misunderstandings that have caused a great deal of concern. Now will you help me, or not?'

'What do I have to do?' She was still intensely suspicious and it showed.

'First off—trust me,' he replied, eyes dark with a seriousness she'd never seen in them before. He reached across the table and took her fingers in his hand, seeming oblivious to the sudden jolt of her pulse as he touched her.

'That's ... asking a great deal,' she replied lightly— and then had to smile to show she was attempting humour, because his eyes darkened even further, and there seemed to be anger there as well. Instead of trying to free her hand, Kaarin cupped it inside his, and said, 'All right, I'll help. Just tell me what to do.'

'Good!' His face brightened and he jumped to his feet and called for the account, which was brought immediately.

A minute later they were on the street, blinking in the bright sunlight, and heading for the car.

'I'll drive, this time. It isn't far,' he said before helping her into the passenger seat and then clambering into the driving seat and adjusting the seat to accommodate his long legs.

'Now, all you have to do is follow my lead. Whatever I say, you go along with it, no arguments, no hysterical giggles—and no running away,' he said as the car spun into the traffic and headed south along Barolin Street.

A few minutes later they were wheeling up beneath the portico of a big two-storey house in a residential street, and Jack seemed lost in thought. He eased out of the car, came around to help Kaarin disembark, then shook one finger in a derisive gesture.

'Damn! I very nearly forgot,' he said, reaching into his jacket pocket and hauling out a small jewellery box. 'Give me your hand, please. Quickly now, or we'll have given the game away.'

She did so, hesitantly, then gasped with astonishment at the enormous blue-fire diamond that he slipped over her ring finger. She started to protest, but her mouth wouldn't work and his hand was gripping her arm tightly as he walked her towards the front door and rang the bell.

She was still trying to speak when the door opened and a kindly-looking woman stood looking expectantly at them. 'You'll be Mr Collier?' she asked politely, stepping aside to usher them inside.

'I am. And this is Kaarin Amos, my fiancée,' Jack replied firmly. The lady nodded at Kaarin, smiled, and led them through to a small, comfortable office with two soft chairs facing a large wooden desk.

But it was the certificate on the wall behind the desk that caught Kaarin's eyes, a certificate that named their hostess, and gave her profession—Marriage Celebrant!

'You'll have to forgive Kaarin's surprise,' Jack was saying then. 'I sort of brought her under . . . well, not exactly false pretences, but close. I'm afraid she's just a bit surprised.'

The lady behind the desk raised one eyebrow and looked sceptically at both of them. 'I would say that's putting it mildly,' she replied. 'Don't worry, my dear. Your . . . fiancée might not be aware of it, but I require a full month's notice before I'm legally allowed to marry you, so . . .'

'I know all that,' Jack interrupted, and then smiled as if in apology for any rudeness. 'Please understand, I'm not trying to trap the girl into anything; I just want her to know and believe that we *are* engaged and that I *do* intend to marry her. It was her idea, you see, and she refuses to believe I've accepted.'

There was a moment's silence—silence in which the marriage celebrant didn't seem able to speak, Kaarin simply couldn't, and Jack was busy fumbling through his pockets for a handful of documents which he subsequently laid on the desk before them.

'I think you'll find everything that's required here,' he said. 'And we'll need a bit more than a month; I'd like to get our new house reasonably well completed, and that'll take—oh, say seven weeks. What do you think, Kaarin?'

'I think that crack on the head has driven you right round the twist,' she said, hearing the words emerge and not even sure if she'd actually said them or merely imagined it all. The room seemed to be spinning around her, and total, stark disbelief had her wide-eyed and totally confused. None of this made any sense.

'There! You see my problem?' Jack exclaimed. 'She just will not believe that I want to marry her.'

'Perhaps if I were to leave you alone for a few moments,' the celebrant said, rising to glide from the room with a somewhat apprehensive glance at Jack, who turned immediately to Kaarin once the door had closed.

Taking her hands in his own, he held her down, easily thwarting her attempts to rise from her chair. When she finally abandoned the effort, he sat, silent and still solid in his grip, until finally she turned to face him.

He stared into her eyes for what seemed like years, seeming to peer past her every defence, past her confusion, her anger, her fear.

'I'm sorry,' he said then, speaking so softly she could barely make out the words. 'I honestly didn't realise it would be such a shock to you. It was supposed to be . . .'

'A pleasant surprise for your best friend in the whole world?' she concluded. 'Or simply the most vicious, spiteful practical joke in the whole world?'

He shook his head sadly. 'No, my love. Never . . . ever . . . that. Just the . . . the most damning error in judgment I think I've ever made. That knock on the head would make a great excuse, but I don't deserve one. All I wanted was to give you a . . . a dramatic exhibition of how much I do want to marry you, and I thought... I was sure that you understood well enough that... but I was wrong and I see that now.'

He stood up, lifting her with him because he simply wouldn't let go of her hands. 'Come on,' he said. 'We'll go now and discuss this properly. I'm sure Mrs... er ... whatshername will understand. And you must understand, too, Kaarin. It's only that I love you so much, so very much. And sometimes it seems to get all lost in the bickering and everything, and...'

Kaarin shook her head, blonde hair flying as everything suddenly fell into perspective, all the clouds of confusion spinning off like so much dawn mist.

'You did all this because you love me and wanted a dramatic exhibition?' she said. 'It wouldn't have been easier to just *tell* me?'

'But I was sure you *knew* I loved you,' he replied. 'It was the marriage part I thought you didn't believe.'

'My darling, crazy man,' Kaarin whispered, rising to touch his lips with her own. 'All I knew was that I loved you, have loved you since... oh, forever. But as for you loving me in return, I could only...'

He stopped her with his own kiss, and it wasn't the fleeting gesture that hers had been. He crushed her to him, moulding her body to his with all the strength in his arms, kissing her until she thought she'd never be able to get another breath.

A tap on the door interrupted them, but when the marriage celebrant stepped into the room she could see enough from their expressions to bring a smile of pleasure to her face.

'I'm so glad to see you've got everything straightened out,' she said, only to be halted by Jack.

'But now that we have, I want to be positive I'm not making a worse mistake,' he said. 'Kaarin, you're sure I'm not rushing you...'

'My only concern is that you won't be fit enough to get started on the building next week,' she laughed. 'I don't mind waiting seven weeks, but I'm darned if I'll wait any more than that!'

The celebrant smiled and began to arrange the various forms that needed to be filled out for the satisfaction of bureaucracy.

Kaarin was in the rock pool when Jack stepped cautiously down the slope from the building site, the white bandage at his crown gleaming in the pale evening light.

'I thought we agreed you weren't going to wear that swimsuit any more,' he growled, easing his tall frame down to a flat rock from which he could watch her glide through the water.

'I certainly don't remember any such agreement,' she retorted. 'Must have been some other girl.'

He scowled at her, and would have looked quite fierce but for the quirky lights of laughter in his eyes. 'Oh, it was you all right,' he said. 'But I suppose now that you're officially engaged you think you've got some kind of amnesty.'

'Oh, no. I just know you don't dare come in here after me until you've had your stitches out,' Kaarin laughed. 'What are you doing here anyway? You're supposed to be in bed.'

'I couldn't sleep,' he replied. 'Are you sure that damned woman said we'd have to wait a whole month before getting married?'

'What? This afternoon you were talking very calmly about seven weeks and now you're cutting it down. I think your head's acting up again, darling.'

'It's not my head. Now come out of there before I come in and get you,' he said, rising to poise himself for a dive into the pool after her.

'Don't you dare!' Kaarin squealed. 'The doctor would have both our hides. And I'm not coming out either, not till I'm ready.'

'Well, don't say I didn't warn you,' he retorted, and

the shorts that were his only garment slid down to fall about his ankles.

'That's deliberate blackmail! No! Don't you dare dive in here, you great oaf! All right, you win. I'll come out,' she shrieked as he moved determinedly towards the edge.

She scrambled for the shore and came dripping to his arms, her lips raised to meet his mouth as it descended and her heart singing at his touch.

'You'd better start work again on the house awfully soon,' she whispered as they strolled together up the hillside.

'Not tonight,' was the whispered reply as his arm tightened around her. 'Tonight I've got better things to do.'

Harlequin Plus
WHAT IS A GORGON?

In Victoria Gordon's *Dream House*, Jack Collier—the hero—tells his friend Bill to send him his "Gorgon"...a most unfair description of the lovely Kaarin, who is anything but a Gorgon.

In classical Greek mythology, there were three Gorgons said to be sisters—Stheno, Euryale and Medusa. Fearsome monsters, they had great wings, long claws and a mass of hideous serpents for hair. So terrible were they that all who dared look upon them turned to stone.

But Medusa had once been a beautiful young woman and thus was the only Gorgon who was mortal. She had been turned into a monster by Athena, goddess of war, handicraft and wisdom. The story goes that Medusa had dallied with Poseidon in Athena's temple, and so outraged was Athena that she turned Medusa into the most frightening of the Gorgons.

It was Perseus, a son of Zeus, who finally slew Medusa with a sword given to him by the god Hermes. Perseus did not turn to stone, for he cleverly looked only at her reflection in Athena's shield while decapitating the creature.

The Gorgon's head was a favorite subject of ancient Greek art. It was believed that even in death, Medusa's head retained its awesome power, and the Greeks carved it on their shields and armor—even on city walls—as a form of protection.

FREE!
Romance Treasury

**A beautifully bound,
value-packed,
three-in-one
volume of romance!**

FREE!

A hardcover Romance Treasury volume containing 3 treasured works of romance by 3 outstanding Harlequin authors...

...as your introduction to Harlequin's Romance Treasury subscription plan!

Romance Treasury

...almost 600 pages of exciting romance reading every month at the low cost of $6.97 a volume!

A wonderful way to collect many of Harlequin's most beautiful love stories, all originally published in the late '60s and early '70s. Each value-packed volume, bound in a distinctive gold-embossed leatherette case and wrapped in a colorfully illustrated dust jacket, contains...

- 3 full-length novels by 3 world-famous authors of romance fiction
- a unique illustration for every novel
- the elegant touch of a delicate bound-in ribbon bookmark... and much, much more!

Romance Treasury

...for a library of romance you'll treasure forever!

Complete and mail today the FREE gift certificate and subscription reservation on the following page.

Romance Treasury

An exciting opportunity to collect treasured works of romance! Almost 600 pages of exciting romance reading in each beautifully bound hardcover volume!

You may cancel your subscription whenever you wish! You don't have to buy any minimum number of volumes. Whenever you decide to stop your subscription just drop us a line and we'll cancel all further shipments.

FREE GIFT!
Certificate and Subscription Reservation

Mail this coupon today to
Harlequin Reader Service

In the U.S.A.
1440 South Priest Drive
Tempe, AZ 85281

In Canada
649 Ontario Street
Stratford, Ontario N5A 6W2

Please send me my FREE Romance Treasury volume. Also, reserve a subscription to the new Romance Treasury published every month. Each month I will receive a Romance Treasury volume at the low price of $6.97 plus 75¢ for postage and handling (total—$7.72). There are no hidden charges. I am free to cancel at any time, but if I do, my FREE Romance Treasury volume is mine to keep, without any obligation.

NAME _____
(Please Print)
ADDRESS _____
CITY _____
STATE/PROV. _____
ZIP/POSTAL CODE _____

Offer expires August 31, 1982
Offer not valid to present subscribers.   D2458